# SHATTERED

THE HOUSE OF CRIMSON & CLOVER VOLUME II

SARAH M. CRADIT

Cover Design by Sarah M. Cradit
Editing by Shaner Media Creations

Publisher Contact:

sarah@sarahmcradit.com

www.sarahmcradit.com

# PRAISE FOR THE HOUSE OF CRIMSON & CLOVER

"Cradit's words flow in prosaic candor like a melody of the ages: pronounced, patient, lingering, and beautiful.

**Dionne Charlet, *New Orleans Examiner***

"Her (Cradit's) talent for creating atmosphere rivals Daphne du Maurier. This is modern Gothic with fierce smarts. Can't say it enough. I loved this book."

**Christopher Rice, *New York Times* Bestselling Author of *The Heavens Rise***

"It takes a great writer like Cradit to weave the threads of so many characters into an enjoyable story. I have no doubt that the name Cradit will one day be associated with the echelon of gothic fiction writers, namely Radcliffe, Blackwood, and Rice."

**Becket, Bestselling Author of *The Blood Vicicanti* and Former Assistant to Anne Rice**

"Sarah Cradit's writing is tight and masterful. Her keen sense of how to pace a book and her ability to use just the right language to express the desires, fears and hopes of her characters is flawless."

**Ionia Martin, Vine Top 100 Reviewer, Readful Things**

"Cradit does an incredible job of building suspense. It's a slow, moody, edge of your seat suspense with a palpable sense of foreboding. This atmosphere kicks the book off and slowly escalates as you sink deeper into it."

**Julie Whiteley, Clue Review**

"The plot flows so quickly that you reach the end of the story well before you are ready and without realizing how much time has gone by since you were enchanted, committed and flung into the world of the Sullivans, Deschanels and their friends. You become a part of their lives as you are reading the books and think about the characters long after you have finished reading the book."

**Stephenee Carsten, Nerd Girl Official**

# ALSO BY SARAH M. CRADIT

KINGDOM OF THE WHITE SEA

Kingdom of the White Sea Trilogy

The Kingless Crown

The Broken Realm

The Hidden Kingdom

The Book of All Things

The Raven and the Rush

The Sylvan and the Sand

The Altruist and the Assassin

The Melody and the Master

The Claw and the Crowned

THE SAGA OF CRIMSON & CLOVER

The House of Crimson and Clover Series

The Storm and the Darkness

Shattered

The Illusions of Eventide

Bound

Midnight Dynasty

Asunder

Empire of Shadows

Myths of Midwinter

The Hinterland Veil

The Secrets Amongst the Cypress

Within the Garden of Twilight

House of Dusk, House of Dawn

Midnight Dynasty Series

A Tempest of Discovery

A Storm of Revelations

A Torrent of Deceit

**The Seven Series**

1970

1972

1973

1974

1975

1976

1980

**Vampires of the Merovingi Series**

The Island

and more

**The Dusk Trilogy**

St. Charles at Dusk: The Story of Oz and Adrienne

Flourish: The Story of Anne Fontaine

Banshee: The Story of Giselle Deschanel

**Crimson & Clover Stories**

Surrender: The Story of Oz and Ana

Shame: The Story of Jonathan St. Andrews

Fire & Ice: The Story of Remy & Fleur

Dark Blessing: The Landry Triplets

Pandora's Box: The Story of Jasper & Pandora

The Menagerie: Oriana's Den of Iniquities

A Band of Heather: The Story of Colleen and Noah

The Ephemeral: The Story of Autumn & Gabriel

Bayou's Edge: The Landry Triplets

**For more information, and exciting bonus material, visit www.sarahmcradit.com**

*For all those who are still searching for their light in the darkness*

*"Deep into that darkness peering, long I stood there, wondering, fearing, doubting, dreaming dreams no mortal ever dared to dream before."*

Edgar Allan Poe

THE
HANGED MAN

# 1

# ANA

Anasofiya Deschanel sat before the antique glass vanity, gazing mournfully at the contents of her cosmetic case. The notion of being on display all night was horrifying, and rather than preparing, as she should have, she pushed it out of her mind until the moment was upon her. Now, her heart and stomach were both a fluttery mess.

Ana successfully avoided the spotlight most of her life. Growing up in one of the most prominent families in New Orleans, her father Augustus graciously protected his only child, accepting her innate discomfort with society life. He wasn't so different himself. He'd taken a backseat for years, letting his sister, Colleen, run the family when their older brother, Charles, died.

When she did need to put on a brave face, Nicolas was a comforting distraction from her unease. But this was not New Orleans. Nicolas and her father were not here.

When Ana proposed the restoration of the Casco Bay Lighthouse, she assumed it would be a simple matter, her father giving the nod to his accountant. She hadn't foreseen the outpouring of appreciation and warm wishes from Summer Island, Maine's two hundred residents—people who had recently been so cold and unwelcoming—nor that Mayor Cairne would join forces with the city of Portland to host a celebration aboard the Grand Atlantic.

*It won't be nearly as unpleasant as you're expecting,* her father promised, when the invitations went out. *In any case, your attendance is perfunctory this time, as my schedule isn't flexible, sweetheart.*

Ana suspected he could've moved things around, had he truly wanted to. He was punishing her, for her decision to stay in Maine with Finn. Her father had somehow resisted being overly critical of her decision not to join the family business, but apparently drew the line at his daughter dating a lobsterman. It didn't seem to matter that Finn had turned a hobby into a successful business venture, just like Augustus had, once upon a time.

In light of her father's displeasure, Ana had expected him to bargain with her when she proposed the restoration; to request she come home, in exchange. But when she spoke to him on the phone about it, he hesitated for only the briefest of moments before agreeing.

*If this puts the Alex Whitman issue to bed, consider it done,* he'd said.

Ana didn't think anything could do that. Alex hadn't only terrorized her, Finn, and Jon, but his sadistic behavior had left a lingering mark on every resident on the island. No one would've guessed quiet, unassuming Alex Whitman was responsible for the four unsolved murders that ravaged the small community over the years. Ana wouldn't have suspected it either, had he not come after her with the same single-minded determination. She was incredibly fortunate to be alive. Finn too.

Alex was gone now, a single shot to the head ending his reign of terror on Summer Island. Following the showdown at the St. Andrews house, Ana and Finn spent several weeks in the hospital convalescing. Ana recovered first. She was a healer, after all, even if this unique ability usually only worked on herself. Most Deschanels were born with unusual talents, or "gifts" as they called them, and she'd never been more grateful for hers. Finn's recovery took longer, his wounds being more grievous. *Yes, but he's alive, at least in part because of you,* she reminded herself. *He's the first person you've ever been able to heal other than yourself. That means something.*

Perhaps it did, but Finn wouldn't have been shot to begin with if she'd never come to Maine, running from her personal demons.

The mirror filled with Finn's kind face, smiling back

at her. Ana nearly jumped. Lost in her reverie, she hadn't heard him come in. "We have to leave in ten," he said, kissing the top of her head. "Everything okay?"

Ana nodded, smiling to push away the dark memories.

"You look..." Finn cocked his head, parting his lips in contemplation. "Beautiful? No, that's not quite right."

"Horrified?" Her strained face stared back from the mirror.

"I'm not a fan of crowds either," Finn commiserated. Mindlessly, he pulled her red hair back from her face, twisting it in his hands, before letting it fall softly across her bare shoulders. "But you're a local hero now, Ana. Hell, I bet you don't even pay for your own drinks tonight!"

Ana laughed at the scandalized expression he made in the mirror. "That's clearly the watermark for the big time," she agreed. Setting her misery aside for a moment, she allowed herself to really look at him, something normally reserved for when he slept peacefully beside her.

Finn was beautiful. He was tall, built strong and sturdy, for the sea. His blonde hair grew darker as the winter wore on, but his blue eyes were as bright as his beloved Atlantic. Behind them, a sea of imagination, and thoughts unspoken. For all his skill with his hands, Finn had an equally gifted mind, possessing endless curiosity about the world around him.

Though, none of those qualities were what Ana

loved most. With Finn, she was accepted, safe, and loved unconditionally. With Finn, she could be herself.

Seeing him in the black tux that once belonged to his father, Ana thought he looked like the perfect gentleman. *There are many, many sides to Finnegan St. Andrews.*

Ana was so unprepared for the event, shopping for a dress hadn't occurred to her until that morning. The mainland was an hour on the ferry, so she rummaged through her mother's closet, hoping to find something suitable. What she found was mostly cable knit and corduroy, but she eventually discovered an old, strapless blue evening gown, wrapped in dusty plastic, hiding in the back.

*This could work.* The only problem was the size of the tailored gown. Ana's mother had been more petite than her daughter, with the spindly limbs of a ballet dancer. Ana was lean, but developed in areas her mother hadn't been. She feared one wrong move might leave either her top, or bottom exposed, for all of Summer Island's fine citizens.

"Like a Celtic princess," Finn concluded, as he watched her thoughtfully in the mirror, his blue eyes widening. "Yes, that's it."

"Stop," she demurred, the blush rising to her cheeks genuine. "I need to finish getting ready."

"Of course. Can you check my tie real quick?" he asked, leaning over her.

She eyed him suspiciously. “It looks fine, but you knew that.”

Finn produced a single strand of freshwater pearls, slipping them from his front pocket. As he reached behind her neck to secure them, his youthful smile widened. “Guilty. But it was more fun than just handing these to you. They were my mother’s.”

Ana admired the heirloom in the mirror, smiling despite her ill humor. She knew what Finn’s mother had meant to him, what these must also represent. Her voice caught in her throat as she whispered, “Thank you.”

Finn’s face erupted into a spirited, sly grin, as he added, “*Aaand*, it was a great way to snag a glimpse down that slightly ill-fitting dress of yours.”

Ana playfully swatted him away, but he snuck in a cheek kiss. “I’ll ask Jon to warm up the car,” Finn said. As he reached the door, he winked at her reflection and mimicked dropping his trousers. When he saw her eyebrows raise in the mirror, he laughed and left. He always knew how to bring a smile to her face, no matter the darkness in her heart.

After he was gone, her smile faded.

Jonathan.

She’d forgotten him for a few, peaceful moments. On top of everything else, he’d be a constant presence tonight, when what she most needed was peace.

# 2

## ANA

The Grand Atlantic was a far larger vessel than required for the Casco Bay Lighthouse Restoration Gala, capable of accommodating ten times the number invited. In offering its use, the mayor of Portland showed a rare generosity toward Summer Island. The big city had all but ignored the remote island community for the last twenty years.

"Ms. Deschanel, that dress does so bring out the blue in your eyes," Mayor Cairne said as he escorted Ana into the ballroom. Rather than putting her at ease, the compliment made her retreat further into herself. The gown had seemed benign enough, but judging from the looks she received as she moved across the floor, she'd miscalculated in some way.

But running away wasn't an option. She was the guest of honor, for a cause she believed in. So, Ana smiled and tucked away the darkness as she was led around the room, from guest to guest. Introductions were made, and Ana found herself enjoying affable conversation with the same citizens who'd once snubbed her when she arrived in the community. The irony wasn't lost on her, but dwelling on it, or harboring resentment, only put a finer point on her discomfort. Instead, she flashed them her winning Deschanel smile, and put forth an effort that would have made her father proud.

Finn's strong hand at her waist served as an unexpected comfort. *Since when has a man's presence soothed me like that?* Other than her cousin Nicolas, never. But she couldn't rely on Nicolas for security anymore. Not after what happened. All her calls and emails to him remained unreturned, and her wounded heart didn't expect that to change.

To her left, Finn was laughing and telling stories, doing more than his share of keeping guests engaged as they mingled. Every now and then, he tossed her a conspiratorial wink, or a subtle hand squeeze. He didn't enjoy large social affairs any more than she did, but he was doing it, and well. For her.

In only a handful of weeks, Finn knew her better than the majority of her own family. His kindness made her heart swell, lighting within her an affection unknown since her teenage years. It happened so swiftly, and unexpectedly, that Ana still struggled to define it.

Jonathan, however, was the antithesis to his spirited

younger brother. His lanky, dark features melded with the dismal brown suit he wore, his sulking expression an unattractive accessory to an entirely glum visage. He looked on the outside the way she felt on the inside, though she had the manners to overcome her peculiarities for the sake of others.

It wasn't clear if Jon had simply never learned how to set aside his inner darkness, or had never cared enough to try. Eyeing his thoughtful, fun-loving younger brother, Ana guessed it was more the latter.

Nearly every interaction she had with Jon was unpleasant. Something fundamental had shifted in the weeks following the incident with Alex, where they'd all worked together to survive the ordeal. Even after, as they nursed Finn to health, side by side, he'd warmed to her, which was unexpected, but nice. She'd have called him her friend.

That was all in the past now. When she had the misfortune of being in his proximity, he either peppered her with passive-aggressive jabs, or had the audacity to pretend she didn't exist at all. Rude people were nothing new to Ana, but Jon exerted a significant amount of energy into being as ill-humored as possible, where she was concerned. He made everything harder than it needed to be.

Ana had seen a part of herself in Jon; a sliver of light, unsure how to break free from its murky crypt. And he'd seen it in her, as well. In one intense moment, these realizations bubbled to the surface, resulting in a senseless act of desperation that never, ever should have happened.

With the benefit of distance from the foolish encounter, Ana had time to reflect on what it meant. She now understood Jon was a physical manifestation of the darkness she lived with, inside her, all her life. In his arms, she'd momentarily clung to the hopeful possibility of someone who might understand who she was. But while she fought her darkness, knowing it would inevitably destroy her, Jon stewed in his, feeding negativity, anger, and hostility.

Finn was already developing feelings for Ana when she and Jon had their ill-fated encounter. Jon and Ana never told him what happened that night.

Neither of them was able to forget it, though, and each manifested their regret in polarizing ways. As Ana grew closer to Finn, the knowledge of her betrayal, despite having done nothing wrong, as she and Finn weren't a couple yet, slowly spread through her like a cancer, pervading nearly every waking moment. Her tryst with Jon was yet another lapse in judgment, and she agonized over how it reflected on her chance at future happiness. And how it might affect Finn, should he find out.

Jon, in contrast, chose to channel his feelings into hurtful projections. Ana suspected while what she felt was remorse, Jon instead was experiencing rejection. His words were often cruel, and intentionally cutting, to disguise his bruised feelings.

*I want to move on. He doesn't. He's punishing me for not returning his feelings.*

As the mayor approached the podium, and everyone moved toward their seats, Ana snagged her heel on the side of a chair. The chain reaction sent her careening into the lap of the mayor's wife, Adalynn. Horrified, Ana released a slew of apologies, while Mrs. Cairne laughed it off. As Ana righted herself to walk away, Jon whispered, so just the two of them could hear, "Maybe you should stick to jeans and sweaters."

From anyone else, the words would have been good-natured teasing, but this was only one of many barbs Jon had been throwing at her the past few weeks, reminding her she didn't belong here, and was unwelcome. All it would take was a brief talk with Finn to stop it, but that would open the box wider. Relief from Jon's emotional battery wasn't worth seeing Finn hurt.

"Helpful advice for a black tie affair," she replied.

Jon's eyes and mouth narrowed into a cutting scowl as he noticed the pearls. He was the only man Ana knew who could speak entire sentences with his frown. "Those were my mother's."

"Finn insisted I borrow them," Ana replied, uneasily, scanning the room for the man who'd so tenderly placed them around her neck.

"He shouldn't have. They were meant to be given to the woman he'd marry, not his most recent amusement."

He pushed past her, bee-lining for his seat.

"That was an impressive tumble," Finn teased, rejoining her, with all the playfulness his brother's voice had lacked. He entirely misunderstood her appalled expression, no doubt thinking her still embarrassed over what happened with the mayor's wife. "I would've given it a ten, because the dismount was fluid, but you botched the landing, so that knocks it down to an even eight."

Ana smiled in spite of herself. *You can't let Jon get to you. It's what he wants.* "Actually, I'd say I nailed the landing," she joked back, letting him guide her to their seats. Her place card was located between Finn's and Jon's, but she maneuvered Finn to the middle seat, so she could put as much distance as possible between herself and his dreadful brother.

For the next two hours, Ana sportingly endured the presentations, speeches, and applause. She even managed to make her way to the podium for a few words of her own. While it was far less than they expected from their benefactor, privately, she was proud of herself. The last time she stood in front of this many people had been her college graduation, but Nicolas had been there to ease her through it. *And now you have Finn's loving hands and warm smile.*

As the evening's activities wound down, and hours' worth of alcohol consumption eased everyone to a lull, Ana's spirits slowly improved. The bubbles in the champagne peeled back her self-consciousness, and she even found herself joining in on Finn's silly jokes. Inevitably, the conversation eventually shifted back to the topic *du jour*.

"It's no secret the designer of the lighthouse was a known perv," Jackson McElroy, one of Finn's childhood friends, remarked knowingly. "I mean, look at the thing. No joke necessary." Everyone laughed, except Jon.

"I remember the first time I saw the lighthouse," Ana recalled, dreamily, holding a fluted glass in one hand. Her other hand dangled the uncomfortable heels she'd long since removed. "I thought it was shaped a little bit like..." she trailed off, remembering her audience.

Finn finished his beer and leaned back in his chair. His tie hung off to the side; a couple of shirt buttons had come undone. "Girl, just say it. The damned thing looks like a candy cane dildo!"

Ana laughed into her arm, spilling champagne over her fingers. "Yes! A hideous adult toy."

"How ladylike," Jon muttered, with a downcast roll of the eyes.

Finn briefly gripped Ana's inner thigh, grinning. "I love it when she talks like that."

Jon twisted his lips together, eyes twinkling with dark mischief. "Yes, well, you never were known for your taste."

Finn's smile died, as the color drained from Ana's

face. The air around the small table was sucked out in an instant, as if entering the eye of a storm.

Before anyone could attempt to fill the awkward silence, Ana excused herself for some air.

The chilled breeze rushed up into her face, and the tears froze against her cheeks.

Ana had never before wished so deeply for her mother.

# 3
# FINN

Finn set aside his worn copy of *The Silmarillion*, squinting with disdain at the snow beyond the living room bay window. He loved the holidays as much as anyone, but they were also the worst time of year for a lobsterman. It meant two to three months where he couldn't be out on the sea every day, connecting with nature, being useful. It had been a whirlwind winter, so he managed to stave off cabin fever for longer than usual, but was now beginning to suffer the first itches.

Now that he had Ana, the feeling grew worse, not better. Though he would've loved to throw responsibility aside and spend every waking moment with her, he also felt an innate need to care for her, to provide for her. There was only one way he could do that cooped up indoors. While he lived for those intimate moments with her, he also wanted, and needed, to be strong for her on a fundamental level. He wanted to be more than her lover.

Though it was nearly lunchtime, Ana was still upstairs, resting from the night before. It was unlike her to sleep late, but Finn knew the event had taken a lot out of her. Jon had risen early and gone into his office in town, despite it being the weekend. With only Finn and his dog, Angus, padding around, the St. Andrews home was unusually silent.

*They're both acting so strange,* Finn thought. Jon's unexpectedly cutting remark the night before hadn't been the first indication, either. Lately, his brother formed a habit of leaving a room whenever Ana entered it. And for the past few weeks, since Finn had come home from the hospital, and his relationship with Ana began to evolve, Jon started working late in the evenings and missing dinner.

After they arrived home from the gala, Finn walked in on a conversation between Jon and Ana that was so unbelievably tense he honestly wondered if he might have imagined it.

*I just wanna go to bed,* Ana had said, as Jon towered over where she sat at the vanity, removing her jewels and makeup. *I'm exhausted.*

*It's a simple question,* Jon pressed, arms folded over his chest. He towered over her like a cruel and formidable bully.

Ana tilted her head up at Jon, and from Finn's vantage point, he saw the mascara newly streaking her cheeks. *There's nothing simple about it, Jon. And I don't owe you an answer.*

Jon laughed in such a maniacal, cruel way, it occurred to Finn he might be staring at Jon's evil doppelgänger. *There's nothing here for you, Ana.*

*I disagree,* Ana replied, breaking the stalemate by looking down at her trembling hands. *Please go.*

Wanting to give her time to compose herself, Finn waited until Jon was gone before slipping into the bedroom, but by then, Ana was sound asleep. She remained that way, without stirring, all through the night, into the morning.

As he gazed up the stairs, Finn wondered if broaching the subject with her would help relieve her stress or result in pushing her further away. Ana was an incredibly private woman, and even getting to know basic things about her felt like chipping away at ancient stone.

In the end, Finn chose action over words. Slipping in bed beside Ana, he wrapped his arms around her as he tenderly demonstrated his support in the most sincere way he knew how.

# 4
## ANA

No matter what else she tried to focus on, Ana's mind kept wandering back to the conversation she had with Jon after the gala. He *insisted* on knowing when she was returning home to New Orleans. Though she'd been deliberately evasive when faced with his antagonizing, the truth was, she hadn't decided.

Returning home had always been the eventual goal. But anytime she resolved to do it, Finn's gentle, smiling face dulled her desire to leave. Whether she wanted to admit it or not, her feelings were beginning to establish deep roots. If she was going to leave, she'd need to do it soon, before affection turned to full-fledged love.

Except, it *was* turning to love, whether she was willing to admit it or not.

Months had passed since she left her teaching job at Tulane in New Orleans, enough time that she was beginning to miss it. When Finn showed her the opening in the English department at the University of Maine, a clear indication that *he,* at least, was hoping she would stay, she couldn't deny her interest was piqued. *It doesn't hurt to have a discussion.*

The truth was, she wouldn't even need an interview. One mention of her father, the founder of *Deschanel Media Group*, would get her in, even if her experience at Tulane didn't. But she wouldn't use that reference. Would, in fact, avoid it unless expressly asked.

Jon snuck up behind her, as she worked on her résumé. The printout from Finn lay next to her laptop, and he snatched it up before she could move it.

"That answers my question," he said, standing over her. His figure cast a long, dark shadow which made her feel nearly as disquieted as his unpleasant demeanor.

"I haven't even spoken with them yet," Ana replied, closing her laptop, preventing him from seeing that, too. She didn't need Jon's detailed critique.

Jon let out a sound resembling a laugh, but there was no humor in it. "Talking to them will be a waste of your time, and theirs. We both know how this is going to end."

Ana felt the heat rising within her. She didn't want to take his bait, but neither could she sit back and let him continue to heap his abuse on her. "I'm not gonna have this discussion with you," she said, through gritted teeth.

She moved to pick up her laptop and leave, but Jon

stepped in front of her, effectively blocking her escape. "You're giving Finn false hopes. We both know this can't last."

"Can't?" she asked, the fire flashing in her eyes. "Or you don't want it to?"

Jon smirked, folding his lips together in crude formation. "You're right. I don't want it to. Finn deserves better. You and I aren't ones for commitment."

"You have no remorse for the way you treat others," Ana asserted after a careful pause. "So don't *ever* lump you and I together in the same definition. We're nothing alike."

Jon's smile this time was genuine, though it sent chills racing down her spine. How could she have been so blind to who he really was? She thought they shared the misfortune of being introverted, and misunderstood. She saw now, with painful clarity, Jon was exactly who he portrayed himself to be.

"Don't flatter yourself," he replied, still smiling cruelly. "Being pretty on the outside doesn't change what's inside."

"It was a mistake we *both* made," Ana admitted, shifting uncomfortably. Finn was home, somewhere, and she feared him stepping into the middle of this. Jon seemed oblivious. "But you're the only one determined to dwell on it."

Ana nearly jumped as Cocoa snaked around her ankles in greeting. When Ana arrived on Summer Island, the small cat took up residence on her porch, and never left. Ana fed and cared for Cocoa, but didn't really think of the kitty as hers until the day she witnessed Cocoa get struck by a car. Horrified, Ana raced to Jon's office, forgetting all her qualms over his attitude, thinking only of the sweet little ball of fur in her arms.

Cocoa was alive because of Jon. This thought calmed Ana's rising temper. Somewhere inside of him, there was goodness. She wished he wasn't hell bent and determined to bury it so deeply.

Jon's attention diverted to the ringing phone. Ana took the opportunity to leave the conversation, but as she began to ascend the stairs, he called after her.

"Girls like you don't put down roots, Ana."

*Girls like me would do anything in the world to put down roots. Girls like me wish, more than anything else, that we could form meaningful connections with others, and not be so dark inside. Girls like me already love boys like Finn, and are terrified of destroying them with that darkness.*

Ana ignored the slight and kept walking, but Jon's comment hit the intended mark.

# 5
# FINN

Three days before Christmas, an unexpected warm front passed over the island. After the snow melted, the ground remained icy, but clear. Finn was relieved by this turn of events, as it meant their meeting with the lighthouse inspector would be smoother than originally anticipated.

Ana surprised Finn with her easy competence regarding buildings and contracts. She was able to follow along smoothly as they walked the derelict property, discussing ideas and taking notes.

Finn had some knowledge of construction himself. As a young man, he'd helped rebuild half the town when a fire ripped through Androscoggin Avenue. His father sat on the committee, and so Finn spent his evenings listening to him discuss their challenges with permits, quotes, and materials. He'd hoped his knowledge would be helpful to Ana, but she was holding her own in the exchange.

"It will be April before we can break ground," Mr. Carson, the tall, scrawny inspector, said. "This cliff side will need to be shored up. Right now, it poses a hazard, and it's a shame someone tore those fences down." The man frowned, pointing at the thick, metal poles on the cliff that held only remnants of chain link.

"That's fine," Ana said, rubbing her hands together. Warm front or no, the wind whipped mercilessly through the highest point on the island, and the effect was startling. "Will you have sufficient time to secure the permits and contracts?"

Carson frowned again. "Perhaps. Depends on how many times you call your father, I 'spose."

It was Ana's turn to frown. Finn knew she was wary of her origins, and the way it influenced how others treated her. Her tone was assertive. "Just tell me what you need, Mr. Carson, and I'll see that it's done."

Carson nodded, squinting through his wireframes as he scribbled furiously on his clipboard. "Mhm, and then, let's see..."

"How long until the entire project is finished?" Finn asked, wanting to make at least some contribution to the discussion. He sidled up behind Ana, slipping his arms around her waist. His heart surged at the natural way she leaned back into him, as if she'd been doing so for years.

"Too early to tell," Carson replied, ripping the

carbon copy off his notes, handing them to Ana. He slipped the clipboard in under his heavy winter coat, signaling the end of the tour. "But the office will call you in for a planning meeting. Most likely, a kick-off sometime in February."

Ana nodded, reading through the notes. "Thank you, Mr. Carson. We look forward to working with you."

"Aye," the man replied, tipping his imaginary hat. "The pleasure is all ours, Ms. Deschanel."

"That might be the most adult thing I've ever done," Ana admitted, as she watched the inspector back his truck up, and swing down to the road toward town. "I wish my father was here. I think he'd be proud."

Finn planted a gentle kiss on her neck, listening. Ana so seldom talked about herself that whenever she did, she had his full attention. Every now and then, a glimmer of light would push through the cracks of her armor, offering him an enticing glimpse.

She drew in a long sigh, her breath forming a cloud before her as she exhaled. "I wonder if my mother ever came up here."

Finn knew to tread carefully on this topic. Ana had never known her mother, as Catherine Deschanel died when Ana was an infant. But Finn and Jon had heard the stories. What transpired the summer Catherine spent on this island would always be considered a part of Summer Island legend. By the way Ana idolized her mother, Finn was quite certain she was blissfully unaware of her mother's supposed transgressions. *And I will keep it that way, if I can.*

"Oh, I imagine she did. It's the most beautiful spot on the whole island," Finn assured, letting Ana fall back into his arms again, as she gazed out, toward the choppy Atlantic. Her hair smelled like wind and salt. Like dreams.

"Sometimes I think..." Ana started, but her voice quickly trailed off as she exhaled again, the moment over. Then, she looked at her watch, and turned back toward Finn.

Before she could suggest they leave, Finn folded his arms around her and pulled her close, pressing his lips first to her forehead, then to her lips. "Not just yet," he whispered.

Ana tilted her head back, her wide sapphire eyes gazing up at him. In that moment, the slight breeze pushing her blazing hair back around her face, the soft flush in her pale cheeks, she seemed entirely his. He didn't sense any of her usual anguish. She was Ana, and he was Finn, and there was nothing but the heartening warmth between them, as the dull roar of the waves crashed against the rocks below.

Then it was Ana pressing her lips to his, snaking her arms around his neck as she twined her fingers through his hair. Ana, who pushed him back, toward the large pine tree on the cliff side, her desire for him apparent with every fervent kiss and caress.

Finn imagined this day differently. In the back of his

truck, he had lunch waiting in a small wicker basket, some wine from the Aldridge's vineyard. He didn't know anything about wine, but he knew a girl like Ana, with her breeding, would probably love it. For once, he wanted to take it slow, show her he could be so much more than just her physical comfort.

But Ana was tugging at his pants, so forcefully he worried his belt might snap. Seeing such unexpected passion from her made him forget all about the little basket, and the modest attempt at impressing her. Instead, his blood pulsed with the memory of her legs wrapped around his back, and how her firm full breasts felt pressed against his flesh.

Finn slipped her pants down and she nearly stumbled climbing out of them, but he caught her. He spread his jacket over the rocky ground and lowered her on to it.

Ana's head fell back, her hair dangling off the cliff in fiery waves. She gasped with a start, realizing their proximity to the edge. "I won't let you fall," he whispered, maneuvering over her, silencing her fears with one quick, hungered thrust as he entered her.

"Finn," she cried, repeatedly, as drove himself deeper and faster inside of her. Each time she called his name, his pleasure heightened, and his self-control slipped further away, until he no longer recognized it.

Ana made him forget everything except her.

*Slower,* Finn chided himself, but it was no use. If he closed his eyes and shut out her beautiful, needing gaze he might last longer, but he could not; would not. What he saw in Ana's eyes was reflected in his own soul. This moment wouldn't last forever, but if he lost himself in it, he might be able to hold the memory close inside him, always.

As he neared climax, her own pleasure mounted, and she opened her mouth in a passionate cry as she came beneath him. When she tightened around his cock, Finn spilled immediately, crying out as his body was racked with pulsing shudders.

They both lay there, breaths ragged, remembering the cold. But there were words on Finn's lips, and he wouldn't let them die there.

Placing his hands gently against the sides of her face, he pressed his forehead to hers and whispered, "Ana, this is love. This right here."

She said nothing for the longest time, but then her eyes blinked with pools of tears, and she nodded.

"It is, isn't it?"

# 6

## JON

The tightness in Jon's belly spread to the rest of him, as he watched his brother and Ana. Ana snored softly against Finn's chest, snuggled under one of his arms while he held a book in front of his face with the other. The lights from the Christmas tree cast a colorful glow over the happy couple, magnifying the joy they clearly felt in the presence of one another.

Christmas was right around the corner, but Jon could not be less in the holiday spirit.

He wanted her gone. He wanted her here. He loathed her. He loved her.

Jon was so enslaved by these conflicting emotions he could hardly get through each day. His deep desire for her, when submerged in the knowledge she was not his, quickly turned to a toxic hatred, manifesting in every word, thought, and action.

It didn't help that Finn was so over-the-moon about her. Jon could count on one hand the times Finn brought someone home more than once. Finn had always proudly proclaimed his only love was the sea. Jon now watched, helplessly, as his little brother found a new, more serious love.

*Anyone but her.*

Instead of being happy for his brother, he grew to despise Finn's contented smiles and sighs.

Night after night, Jon was forced to listen to the sounds coming from the room down the hall. If Finn knew Jon could hear, he would've been more discreet, surely, but if Jon broached the topic, the truth and source of his discomfort would be written on his face, plain as day.

Things might have been different if Jon had confronted Ana before she'd fallen for Finn; if he'd simply said what was on his mind, for once. But Jon could not, and would not. He would rather suffer in silence than ever admit he might have feelings capable of bringing him to his knees.

"Dammit," Finn whispered, breaking Jon out of his dark reverie.

Jon turned toward his brother. "Everything okay?"

"Come here real quick." Finn kept his voice low. Jon approached warily, as Finn gestured toward Ana. "Hold her for me a minute. I'll take her to bed, but I need to change my shirt first." Finn motioned toward the cocoa he spilled down the front of his tee.

Jon hesitated, his heart flipping in his chest. "Take it off, I'll give it a rinse in the sink," Jon offered, but Finn rolled his eyes and beckoned him over.

"Just come here!"

Jon approached, knowing he had no other choice. Protesting would look ridiculous, and suspicious. As Finn gently slid her up, Jon settled into his place, and Ana's warm face tumbled against his chest. She murmured something in her sleep, snuggling into him.

Finn jogged toward the laundry room, then turned back. "Actually, take her upstairs. I'll be right there." When Finn saw Jon's expression, he added, "For heaven's sake, it's not the first time you've carried her up the stairs!"

No, not the first time. The first time, he'd saved her life. The second, he'd made love to her.

Jon started to object, but Finn was already gone. He wanted to sink further into the sofa until he disappeared entirely, taking his torment with him.

He saw no choice but to do as Finn asked. Carefully, he stood, lifting Ana's sleeping form into his arms, thinking of the last time he'd held her. *Just a fling*, he would've called it then, but time had a funny way of providing unwanted clarity.

As they ascended the stairs, Ana's warm breath passed through his thin shirt, stirring feelings both above and beneath. When he reached the top, he looked down into the room below. *It would be nothing to drop her; to watch her fall down the stairs, and never wake up. To end this all.*

A lump rose in his throat. That there was such horrid darkness in him, capable of even considering such a thing, appalled him. But it didn't change his feelings.

When he finally reached Finn's room, he settled her into the bed, and moved to leave. Before he could, her arms were around his neck, and she smiled, in a sleepy daze, cooing, "Don't go."

Jon was certain his heart would thump clear out of his chest. *She feels it, too. She understands.* Placing one hand against the side of her face, he leaned forward, pressing his lips softly to hers. As her lips parted, and her warm breath filled his mouth, she whispered, "My Poseidon...."

Nauseating horror filled Jon as he backed quickly away, dropping her arms rudely to her sides. Her eyes fluttered open and for one awful moment they watched each other, wordless.

Before either could break the silence, Finn burst into the room, flashing Jon a goofy grin before throwing himself on to the bed beside Ana.

"Thanks for waking her up, so I didn't have to," Finn said with a wink at Jon, before he rolled atop Ana, inciting a drowsy giggle from her. As Finn frolicked, he seemed to forget Jon was even standing there.

"Don't mention it," Jon said, as he backed from the room, allowing his gaze to linger a moment as Finn's hands searched the body of the only woman Jon had ever really wanted.

Jon closed the door. The sounds from the other side reminded him once again of his revulsion; his darkness. *She has to leave. If there's a way to make her do it, I'll find it.*

Jon hated Ana for not loving him. For taking not only his heart, but his brother. He felt unfathomable loathing for her, for crushing the last of his humanity with her refusal to acknowledge what they shared.

*I'll exploit any weakness I can find, and push her away.*

# 7
# ANA

On Christmas Eve, Ana snuck off to her own house for some privacy. She told Finn she needed to pick up more of her things and check on the house, but as soon as she passed through the tall white door of the old Victorian, she was lost to any productive activity. Outside, a fresh snow fell, blanketing the island.

She left the St. Andrews house in the midst of an argument between the brothers. The fight had nothing to do with her, but she didn't doubt, at the core, her presence was the source. The tension festering between Ana and Jon was spreading now, and soon it would be out of control.

With a great sigh, Ana sunk into one of the kitchen chairs, pressing her face against the old wooden table. She didn't want to think about anyone, or anything. She wished only to take in the old smells, and soft sounds, to be somewhere other than here.

But whether she was here, or back home in New Orleans, her demons would follow. They never rested.

Ana felt someone sit down beside her. She opened her eyes to see Jon, watching her with an unreadable expression.

"What the hell are you doing here?" she demanded.

"You didn't look too good when you left the house," Jon said blandly. His expression was more curiosity than worry, but it surprisingly lacked most of the usual malice. Rather than disarming her, it immediately alerted her suspicions.

"I'm fine," Ana replied, in a tone conveying the opposite. "And anyway, my well-being hasn't been your concern for a while."

"It's not that simple," Jon sighed, his expression pained. He looked as if he might say more, but instead stared ahead, out the window, silent.

"Why are you here?" Ana repeated. Her anger toward him hadn't subsided, but she couldn't decide how to direct it at him, or if it was even worth the effort.

"I don't know," he confessed. "I came for the same reason as you, I'd guess. To get away."

"Not exactly," Ana replied, with a bitter laugh. She was mystified at his solicitous behavior, how he seemingly disregarded his dreadful treatment of her. "I'm here to get away from *you*."

Jon was silent for a moment, as if trying to gauge

whether or not she was teasing. When she didn't smile, he said, "It's complicated."

Ana watched him, warily, her suspicions rising as his words purposefully echoed hers.

"Sometimes," Jon went on slowly, hesitantly, "I say things without really thinking."

"Sometimes?" Ana repeated, not letting him off the hook, despite what seemed like an attempt at apology. She'd endured quite enough torment from him for a weak acknowledgement to suffice.

"I'm not always the best communicator," Jon admitted.

"Look, did you come out here to rattle off vague statements, or did you actually have something productive to say?"

Jon met her gaze squarely. "What would you like me to say, Ana?"

Ana drew in a cautious breath, realizing his question was multi-layered. What *did* she want him to say? "Nothing," she answered. "I've tried to understand your mind. I don't, and I don't want to."

"I never asked you to understand me," Jon argued, childishly defensive. "It's not my fault you're trying to."

Ana felt the familiar rise of blood to her hands and cheeks, as her surprise turned to anger. He was toying with her, again. He didn't come to apologize at all, just to taunt her further... to push her, further, until she caved to his passive-aggressive demands. "You might not take any accountability for your behavior Jon, but it doesn't mean you're not accountable."

Ana sensed an uncomfortable shift in the tone of the room. "I never pretended to be anyone other than who I am. I am who I am, and I can't change it."

"Also an extremely convenient argument for not taking responsibility. Bravo, you've defined your problem and decided to do absolutely nothing about it. You're a regular champion of the introverts. Cape's in the mail."

"And you're a judgmental bitch," Jon seethed. "You want to know what's worse than someone who realizes who they are and can't change? Someone who denies who they are and tries to be something they're not."

"Trying to improve my quality of life is hardly an abhorrent trait," Ana countered, the sound of her own, cruel laughter ringing in her ears. She was past the point of stopping; of censoring. "I do know who I am, but I also know if I want to change, I can. I have."

"You haven't," Jon insisted. "Happiness can be very easily mistaken for desperation."

"Screw you," she spat. "You and I are not the same. Stop trying to force the comparison."

"You're right, we aren't the same, Ana. Unlike you, I would never try to live some fake life just to prove I'm something I'm not. I wouldn't lead a great guy into believing I could give him some kind of actual, sustainable happiness when I knew good and well it wasn't going to last, because I was incapable." He narrowed his eyes at her, steadying his hands against the table.

"Does it make you feel better about accepting your life the way it is, by insulting me about my attempts to change mine, Jon?" Ana rose, knocking her chair over. "I may be imperfect, but I'm not unkind enough to make others feel terrible so I can share my misery."

Jon seized her arm with trembling hands as she tried to walk away. She widened her eyes in exasperated anger, trying to understand his manic expression, which was, as usual, impossible to interpret. "I would never want you to be miserable. I want you to be happy," he said, dropping his voice.

"Then let me!" she cried, tearing free of his grasp. "Stop trying to make me feel like what I'm doing is wrong."

"It *is* wrong," he insisted stubbornly, his eyes trained on hers.

"Tell me why!"

"You know why. Don't make me say it."

Ana made a conscious effort not to read his thoughts. What would it solve? If he was trying to tell her he had feelings, what could she do about them? Whatever she thought she once, briefly, felt for him had turned to loathing. And now, she was falling in love with his brother.

Ana turned and Jon tugged her arm again, softly, turning her. This time, there were tears in his eyes.

"I can't do this with you anymore," she said, the

sight of his pain calming her. "I know who I am. And I really don't need you to keep holding up the mirror to prove your point."

Jon moved closer, gazing down at her. She shot him a warning glance at his unwelcome familiarity, but was stunned by the turn their conversation had taken. She still didn't understand why he was even here, or what he wanted. "But Ana, you can never step away from what's inside you. And eventually you can't help sharing it with others, either."

Ana shook her head. "I used to believe that. Finn accepts who I am. He doesn't need me to change."

"But why settle for acceptance when you can have understanding?" Jon pushed, further narrowing the gap between them.

"I'm not settling," Ana asserted, and she realized the profound truth of her words as they rushed out. "I'm, finally, exactly where I should be."

"Or deluding yourself," Jon countered with a sad shake of his head.

Jon was wrong. The bond she shared with Finn was the first thing that had ever brought her near to peace. It was only this awful secret keeping her from giving herself fully.

Arguing the point with him would be an exercise in frustrating futility. Jon's stalwart determination to punish himself meant he also believed Ana should continue to do the same. And she wouldn't. Not anymore.

"*La douleur exquise,*" Jon said softly, with a sad shake of his head.

"Excuse me?"

"It's French. 'The exquisite pain.' Wanting someone you can't have, and still holding onto hope for it anyway." Jon kissed her as the last words left his mouth. The gesture shocked Ana so fully she froze, locked in suspended animation laced with extreme disbelief. His hands fastened around her, sliding up and down her back in long, ragged strokes, as if he meant to consume her.

Ana's senses returned, as she wedged her hands between their chests. His mouth moved closer to her ear, crushing her against his chest as he forced her arms back to her sides. She attempted to wriggle free, but Jon was stronger than she was. "I'm sorry, but I love you. You might wish I didn't, and maybe I wish it too, but I do and I don't think it'll ever go away."

"This isn't love," Ana rebutted, but then he was kissing her again. *Stop, stop, stop,* she was crying out, in her head, but her attempts to halt his physical assault were matched by his opposing force, greater than her own.

Jon pushed her back with a careless shove. She nearly tripped over the table as he lowered her on to it. He used one arm to steady her, and the other reached behind her head, tangling in her air, holding the kiss together. Her hand found the table as well, and she gripped desperately for the edge, trying to crawl away.

But Jon's weight crushed her as surely as his warped affections.

"Jon, stop," she pleaded. "Stop!"

Jon didn't hear her, or if he did, he refused to acknowledge her cry. The familiar clanking of unbuckling trousers rang in her ears, as she gasped for air. She was pinned so fully against the table, she couldn't even raise a knee in her defense. *He's so lost in the moment he created he can't sense how wrong this is, how terrified I am.*

In a surge of bravery, Ana bit down on his lower lip, crushing the tender skin between her teeth until she felt a sickening pop. Jon's eyes widened in a painful rage, as he pulled her up by the hair and flipped her, smashing her face into the table. She exhaled sharply as her face connected, pushing the air right out of her.

Ana realized, with a terror unlike any she'd known, his earlier kindness was a deception, designed to culminate in this moment. He *wanted* to hurt her.

Jon's breath was hot against her ear; the spittle flew from his lips as he declared, "I know the one thing that will make you leave." His hands tore crudely at her pants, ripping the button as he pooled them at her ankles, not bothering to fully remove them. He brushed a cold hand over her ass, slipping a finger through her panties.

This last invasion shocked Ana so completely she screamed, but then her face was bouncing off the oak table again, and the room swam in and out of focus. She struggled through her daze, but his hand cuffed her neck, pinning and strangling her all at once.

Ana realized if she didn't get through to him soon, he wouldn't be able to stop himself. *Dear God, he might actually do this.* "I'll do what you want... I'll leave... just please don't do this," she begged, the sharp taste of copper filling her mouth.

"I know you will," Jon said, pausing. His voice was clear. Rational. *This isn't a crime of passion. This is the real Jon.* "But I'll have you again before you do."

Ana wept into the table, tears of fear and fury alike sliding into the old wood. She felt as if she was drifting up and away from herself as she kicked and cried out, fighting a battle she began to grasp she couldn't win. When at last he tore her panties aside, pressing his erection against her, she knew—finally accepted—he meant to do it.

"Really?" a voice called from across the room. The realization that the words came from Finn moved through her mind, slowly, as her head and heart throbbed in unison.

Jon jumped halfway across the room at this interruption, and though she couldn't see his face, his shocking gasp rang loudly in the otherwise quiet room. He stumbled as he tugged at his pants, attempting to pull them back up, failing.

Ana wanted to cry, to scream, to explain, to be silent. She couldn't make up her mind, and she was frozen now, as she was when Jon first began his assault.

Finn's accusatory words sounded like a child experiencing their first true betrayal, his voice filled with raw, innocent hurt.

She started to cry out to Finn in relief, but he didn't see the fear in her eyes. All he saw was his brother and girlfriend, locked in embrace.

Finn crossed his arms, his gaze shifting from one to the other. His stance was colored with anger and control, but his eyes spoke of the pain within.

Without saying anything else, he turned and left.

Ana gasped, bracing herself against the table. Jon was already out the door and after his brother.

# 8

## FINN

As Finn stormed away from Ana's house, toward nothing, he was consumed with a range of emotions mostly foreign to him.

He wanted to be angry, but more of a surprise was the realization his predominant emotion was raw, incomparable pain. Infidelity was almost unforgivable in his eyes, and he always said if ever had the misfortune of being wronged in such a manner, he'd leave and never look back. But that was before, when he had the luxury of opinion instead of experience. Before he met Ana, before he truly loved her the way he did. And this was not just about his love for her, but his brother. His goddamn *brother*!

And Jon's words about having her again... again? So this happened before? How many times? Finn could've stayed, could've asked so many questions, but he was completely emasculated standing before them. Walking away was the only power he had left.

Finn had to admit, the start of their relationship was somewhat unorthodox. Starting with only a kiss and a night of bearing their souls to one another, he'd then fallen in love while nursing her back to health, sharing parts of himself with her, talking to her unconscious form for hours, sleeping by her side. He'd never done anything like that for a woman. Had never wanted to.

But after she woke, through the shootings and subsequent recovery, he grew to know and understand Ana. Her peculiarities weren't a turnoff, but instead another thing about her to love, to protect. It gave him a sense of purpose in a way nothing else in his twenty-seven years ever had, not even the sea.

As he came to know her more deeply, he realized something about her was familiar. Her darkness wasn't so different from Jon's. Finn wondered if he was the only one who saw it.

But Jon projected a cold indifference toward Ana. And Ana was so good to Finn he never felt a reason to be concerned or jealous of anyone, let alone Jon.

As Finn blindly trudged on, the questions in his head raged, unanswered. Why was Ana even with him, anyway, if she had a thing for Jon? It didn't make sense. She *seemed* happy. He didn't *think* she was acting. Even now, after what he'd seen, he still couldn't believe she didn't care for him. But what kind of person could she possibly be, if she would do this to him? With his own fucking brother? His *brother*.

"Finn, wait!" that same brother called from behind him. Finn didn't want to wait. He wanted to pretend he couldn't hear Jon, that Jon didn't exist. Jon, the older brother he'd defended, loved, and protected all these years. The brother he'd given up so many things for, and then sheltered him even from the knowledge of those sacrifices. Finn had never been bitter about any of it, until now.

Finn continued his brisk walk toward Heron Hollow Road, ignoring the sound of his brother jogging to keep up. He had no words adequate for whatever conversation Jon planned to initiate. No patience.

Then Jon grabbed his wrist and spun him around, forcing them face to face. "You need to hear me out," Jon insisted.

"I don't *need* to do anything!" Finn jerked his hand away, and before he could produce a rational thought, that same hand became a fist, and then he was swinging it, full force, into Jon's face. Blood splattered through the snow in a long, grotesque arc, as Jon fell back into the fresh powder.

Looking down at his brother, Finn wanted to do it again, and again. Wanted to wipe the look of hurt surprise off his traitorous face. "You have no right to ask anything at all of me," Finn berated. "Not one damn thing."

Jon buried his face in his shirt, but the blood quickly

stained through the plaid, large dark drips making a pool of red in the snow. "Jesus Christ, Finn. Please, just listen."

"What can you tell me that I don't already know? The two people in this world I care most about betrayed me, at the same time!" But Finn did have questions. He didn't understand the history, and how it had come to this point. He couldn't grasp the scope of the treachery, and while he wasn't sure he wanted to, he needed to.

Eventually.

"Finn!" Ana cried, as she caught up. "Please—"

"You," Finn rebuked, not bothering to squelch the coldness seeping into his words. He couldn't look at her, couldn't allow himself to be calmed by her pretty eyes. "I never want to see you again."

Ana's breaths were ragged, heavy. "Jon, tell him!"

"Tell me what?" Finn demanded.

"Goddammit, Jon!" Ana pleaded. Finn heard the sadness and desperation in her voice. He didn't understand it. He refused to look at her. "Why are you doing this?"

"You two can take your lover's quarrel elsewhere. I'm done," Finn spat. Before he turned to leave, he allowed himself a glance in her direction. "You were right to warn me about you, Ana. I guess this is my fault?"

Ana's shocked face moved from an angry Finn, to a suspiciously quiet Jon. And then, just like that, her expression was blank, as if she'd forced her emotions into a box. “No, it’s mine,” she said after a careful pause, then turned and left.

Finn watched her walk away, feeling as if he was missing something essential, but then Jon was staring at him curiously, with a look of panic mingled with horror.

“You really love her?” Jon asked, in vague wonder.

“You care about that, do you?” Finn’s sarcasm had a knife’s edge.

Jon’s expression continued to crumble, as he seemed to be coming to a very important realization. “What you saw,” he said, gesturing back to toward Ana’s house, “was the end of a discussion long overdue—”

Finn laughed, folding his hands over the top of his head, fearing if he left them hanging he might throw another punch. “Discussion? You and I have far different definitions apparently!”

“Listen. Before you and Ana were together, we had a thing. One time. That was it. It never went further.”

Finn was completely stunned. “When? Tell me when it happened.”

“Before you two were together.”

“No, when *exactly*. I want to know *exactly when you fucked my girlfriend*.”

“She wasn’t your girlfriend—”

“*Tell me*!”

Jon paused. For someone so eager to get the truth out moments ago, he seemed to have lost his enthusiasm. Finally, in an awkward staccato of details, the ugly truth was laid bare. "During the storm, when you went to go find food in the snow cat. She woke up. She was, I don't know, disoriented, and I was overwhelmed. She had a night terror. You know she sleepwalks, I'm sure. I found her outside in the snow, nearly frozen to death. By the time I got her back to the house, we were both close to hypothermic. I ran us a hot shower and... and it just *happened*, Finn. Neither of us planned it. The whole thing is still a blur to me."

Finn listened, unaware his jaw had gone slack during the telling. The one and only time he'd left her bedside, she'd awaken and it was Jonathan's face she saw. It didn't matter that Finn had been holding her hand the entire time. She must have assumed it was Jon all along. Finn's heart sank.

"How could you not tell me?" Finn moaned. Some of his anger had deflated, leaving him feeling simply lost.

"How could I? You started a relationship with her. What was I supposed to say?"

"So what was that just now, then? You two were having a *discussion*?" Finn challenged. His anger returned, rocketing him back and forth between his volatile mood swings.

"Yes," Jon said weakly. "It wasn't what it looked like. Please, let's go home and talk." His eyes, looking over a wad of shirt, were pleading for a chance to explain.

Finn ignored his brother, instead choosing to

remember the moment on the cliff, in front of the lighthouse. *This is love. This right here,* he'd said.

*It is, isn't it?*

Though penetrating her thoughts had been an uphill battle, Finn could always sense the truth behind her eyes. And he'd seen it that day. Ana loved him. She may be confused about a lot of things, but not that.

But Finn wasn't sure if it mattered anymore. He needed to get away, from Jon, from Ana, from all of it. To think, before his head and heart simultaneously exploded into a million little pieces.

"I can't pretend to understand you at all," Finn said finally, in a low, trembling voice. "I've tried, God knows I have, but I just don't. Fuck you for what you've done to me, your only brother. I've done nothing but try to be there for you, and the only time I've ever really cared about someone, you ruined it, because, once again, your feelings mattered more."

Finn turned and continued walking toward the road, away from his brother. He knew Jon wouldn't follow. He could sense his brother's unsaid words trailing behind him, but Finn didn't need to hear them. He didn't want to know anything anymore. This raw, incomparable hurt pierced his heart and made him regret ever giving it away.

FINN WALKED THE MILE INTO TOWN, FINDING HIMSELF IN THE Thirsty Wench. Before, when he'd had nothing to come home to, the Wench had been his regular watering hole. Most of his friends still made their way there several nights a week, and certainly some of his old conquests, too. But sex was the last thing on Finn's mind. It was Christmas Eve, anyway. Most of the townies would be with their friends and family. As Finn should've been.

To his surprise, he saw a familiar face at the end of the bar: Jackson, his old buddy from high school. Jackson was a good guy, one of the few men Finn still regularly associated with. A family man. His wife, Andrea, was once an old girlfriend of Finn's, too, but that was the kind of thing you expected in a community this small.

"Where are Andi and the kids?" Finn asked, taking the stool next to him. Calvin, the bartender, poured Finn a whiskey from memory.

"Portland, to spend the evening with her family," Jackson answered. He played with his napkin, which appeared to have been folded and refolded a hundred times. "Her father and I don't get along so well, and Andi and I have been together so long she doesn't try to force it anymore." Jackson laughed, swirling the clear liquid in his glass. "Didn't expect to see you here, though. Where's that pretty girl of yours?"

Finn wasn't keen to talk about his feelings, but his head swam with the consuming urge to send his fist through the nearest object, and he realized he needed to get all he saw off his chest before it burst completely through. “She’s been fucking Jon,” he blurted, taking a long, measured sip of his whiskey, enjoying the sharp burn as it passed down his throat. Physical pain, he welcomed.

“What? Are you serious?” Jackson shook his head, the surprise on his face mirroring Finn’s own. “Jesus. I’m sorry, man. Didn’t see that coming.”

“Me either,” Finn replied, distantly, still thinking of the afternoon at the lighthouse.

“How’d you find that out?” Jackson asked.

“I saw them together,” Finn responded, and both men cringed in unison. “Jon tried to say they were just talking, but I know what talking looks like. You don’t talk with your pants down.”

“His pants were down?”

“I’d just as soon forget that detail,” Finn said drily, wincing as he drained his whiskey. He had, in fact, blocked out *every* detail, fearing the lack of boundaries with his rage, that he might go home and murder his brother.

Jackson nodded. “What else did he say?”

Finn shrugged. “That it happened before we were together. I should’ve known something was up, with how weird they’d both been acting lately.”

“Oh,” Jackson replied, looking thoughtful. “I mean, if I’d screwed Andi’s sister before her, I don’t know that I’d have told her about it. That’s just asking for an unnecessary fight.”

“Unnecessary?” Finn blinked incredulously. “You

don't think Andrea would have a right to know you slept with her sister?"

"Well, a right, perhaps. But not a reason. What happens before you're with someone doesn't concern them. She'd be angry, when I hadn't done anything wrong. Would create problems for no reason."

Finn knew there was truth in his words. But logic and emotions didn't play well together, and it didn't change what he'd seen tonight. "I don't believe it was just once. I mean, I saw what I saw back there. And you know, I've never seen Jon chase after a woman. When I saw him with her, it was just... surreal."

Jackson finished off his drink, accepting another from the bartender. "Finn, I'm gonna say something I'll ask forgiveness for later, and hope you'll remember how much I had to drink before you hold it against me." Without pausing to wait for Finn's approval, he continued, "Jon is an asshole. I know you don't like hearing that. I remember how many fights you got in when we were younger, defending him."

Finn said nothing.

"But he doesn't deserve your blind loyalty," Jackson continued. "I know you think he does, and you're his brother, so I expect you'll always think he does. But everyone else on this island knows who he is. He treats everyone like shit, and acts like he's the only one entitled to be that way." Jackson leaned in, then, as if he didn't want the bartender, the only other person in the building, to hear. "People loved your Ma and Pa. And they love you. *That's* the only reason people tolerate Jon. And that's the God's honest truth."

Finn looked down at the napkin he didn't realize he'd been shredding. It was true. All his life, he'd defended Jon. No one else understood his brother, and while Finn didn't either, exactly, he at least believed, deep down, Jon was a good person. A kindhearted individual who simply didn't know how to interact with the world around him.

But Ana was like that too, no? Did that not make her the same? Was he wrong about her as well?

"I'm sorry to say those things about your brother," Jackson added, taking Finn's lack of response as anger. "I know how you care about him."

"Don't be," Finn dismissed his apology, slowly, as more and more of his own thoughts began to converge and make sense. "You're right."

Finn had long ignored Jon's seeming lack of compunction for how he treated others, instead choosing to believe his intentions were good. But as Finn thought about the last few weeks, replaying all the moments between himself and Jon, and Jon and Ana, Finn began to answer his own question about Ana. When he compared Jon's actions to Ana's, what he saw in Jon was a spiteful hatred pronounced through his every word and action. In Ana, Finn saw pain.

He saw remorse.

Jon and Ana were not so alike, Finn realized. Where Jon gravitated toward this darkness, feeding off it, Ana was terrified of hers. She'd come to Summer Island to escape it. She'd made a mistake, and Jon punished her for trying to move on. Not because he wanted her, but because he hated her for not wanting him.

Finn finally allowed himself to process the events at Ana's house, and as he did, horrifying details came back to him. The way Jon's hand pressed against the back of Ana's neck. *Not consensual.* The blood on her lips and forehead that he'd seen from the corner of his eye as she walked away. Jon's skittish swing of emotions.

*Jesus, how did I not see these things? How was my rage so blind I missed them? She tried to tell me.*

And Finn had left her like that, alone, after telling her he never wanted to see her again.

"You all right?" Jackson asked, leaning his head to meet Finn's downcast eyes.

"I'm sorry for running off at the mouth like that, Jack," Finn said, remembering himself. He'd known Jackson since they were running around in diapers, but this was the most serious discussion that had ever passed between them.

Jackson waved him off. "If you want my advice, don't talk to Jon. Talk to your girl. What she has to say might surprise you. And, for what it's worth, when I met her, I had a good feeling about her. Not like Jon."

No, not like Jon. Nothing like him, in fact, and Finn was shocked at the contrast his mind now created when comparing the two. Ana came to Summer Island to escape the person she feared she was becoming. Jon remained there because it meant he never had to change.

The last few weeks converged in crystal-clear clarity. The tense conversations between Jon and Ana. Ana's emotional withdrawal whenever Jon was around. Finn *finally* understood, and this revelation was so powerful it was enough to divide his feelings keenly between love for Ana and hatred for his brother. Ana made a mistake and wanted to move on. Jon, in his refusal to let her, was not only destroying her but also her ability to give herself fully to Finn.

Worst of all, Jon's violence toward Ana was utterly unforgivable.

Jackson was right again. It was Ana he needed to see. To give her comfort, to somehow, if he could, right this terrible wrong. And if Jon crossed his path before he could get to her, then Finn couldn't be held accountable for what might happen.

# 9
# JON

All his life, Jon had considered his eccentricities with a vague detachment. He knew he was different, and that these differences challenged him socially; challenged others in their dealings with him. He gave up having a wide array of friends, or being well-liked, and missed out on many opportunities, the kinds others insisted he would regret later. But he never did.

The truth was, Jon never regretted once who or how he was until the moment he saw the pain in his little brother's face. Pain caused, entirely, by his actions.

He'd allowed himself to be intentionally blind to the changes Finn was going through. It was easier to dismiss Finn's emotions as confused, than to believe he was actually falling in love with Ana. Certainly easier to justify Jon's own treatment of her, and his mission to persuade her to return home, or anywhere, as long as

Jon never had to see her again and be faced with how he felt.

Ana wasn't one of Finn's passing fancies, though. Somehow, Jon *had* known that, which made his self-delusions even more of a betrayal. In fact, it was this innate realization that made Jon want her gone, even more than his spiteful, unrequited love.

But what scared Jon most of all, was that he didn't regret, not one bit, the hurt he'd caused Ana. He knew it didn't bode well for his soul, that he would have finished their "conversation" if Finn hadn't walked in.

JON HEARD FINN BEFORE HE SAW HIM. THE YELLING FROM next door carried through the cold, still air, a reverberating reminder of Jon's sins. Finn pleaded with Ana to open her door, to talk, but his continued entreaties went unanswered. As Jon listened, his mouth throbbed with the pain of Ana's terrified bite. It would remind him of his actions for weeks to come.

An hour or so later, Jon heard the back screen door slam. There was nothing Jon could say to his brother that would be adequate, and so instead he remained standing before the Christmas tree, staring at the now garish lights taunting him with irreverent blinks. The unopened presents beneath told of a happiness and togetherness that now seemed so far away.

"I know what you did," Finn accused. He stood, red-faced and dripping of fresh snow.

"Finn—"

"I know what you did, *Jon*!" Finn's voice boomed, as melting snow flew off him in shudders. "What I don't know is *why*!"

Jon was silent for a long time. "I don't know, either," he replied.

Finn snorted in derision.

Jon's love for Finn, and hatred for Ana, burned with an even heat. But he understood he would have to dull his hatred for her to feed his love for his brother. He owed Finn the truth, even if it meant Jon would suffer further.

He took a deep breath, and let the words flow before he changed his mind. "I wanted to punish her for being able to forget that night so easily, when it's all I can think about. I wanted her to know that same rejection when things didn't work out between the two of you. I wanted to..." Jon choked on these last words, "Ruin her for you."

"Ruin her?" Finn repeated, as the words settled over him, slowly.

"I didn't realize how much you cared for her," Jon said, tripping over his apology. The anxiety built within him, slowly, but enough to remind him how close he was to losing control again. "I thought she'd just *leave*, and we could go back to how things were. That it would be like she never came here to begin with. God, Finn, I never meant to hurt you like this. You're my little brother."

"Me?" Finn repeated. The knuckles of his fists bulged, clenched near his thighs. "What about her? What about Ana?"

Jon couldn't tell the truth about this part. Could never say that, despite Finn's pain, Jon wished he'd accomplished his goal, driving her far from Summer Island and both of them. "I wasn't thinking."

Finn moved toward him, and Jon flinched, thinking, for one terrible moment, Finn was going to beat him to a pulp. He'd seen what Finn's hands could do in a rage. Earlier, for the first time in their lives, he'd felt it for himself.

Finn shook his head. "You think I'm going to kick your ass? I should. God knows you deserve it. But that would make me no better than you, and I *never* want to be like you." Finn inhaled, steadying. "Laying hands on a woman. That isn't darkness, Jon. That's fucking sickness. You're sick. And I am *not* your little brother. Not anymore."

Jon didn't move an inch as he watched Finn storm up the stairs. He stayed standing before the hearth as he heard the bathroom door slam, and then creaking from the pipes as the shower turned on. He remained in place long after the water turned off, and Finn retired to his room.

Then there wasn't a sound in the entire house, except the grandfather clock in the dining room, ticking as it counted down Jon's sins.

# 10
## FINN

Finn lay on his bed, unable to sleep. The alcohol had long since worn off, and his head throbbed with the stress of the day. Next door, the only woman he'd ever loved was hurting, but she didn't want his comfort.

He would've slept on her porch if he thought it might help get through to her, but forcing the issue would only push her further away. He'd had his chance to listen, and instead, he let rage guide him.

Images of Ana's bleeding face, and heavy eyes, tortured him all through the night. Every couple of hours, he'd brave the cold and trudge next door, trying, and failing, to appeal to her. At one point he picked up the phone to call Sheriff Horn, but then cradled it again. She might never forgive him for involving someone else in this mess. He wanted to help her, not make her worse. Involving the authorities was her decision to make, and hers alone.

Early Christmas morning, he bundled up, determined to persevere through Ana's defenses. As he walked through the snow, toward her house, it felt like a dense fog had lifted from his heart, allowing him to see the contents in full clarity. *This is love. This right here.* He'd known it the moment he saw her first walk toward him on the beach, clutching that upside down book to her chest. Felt it the first time his lips connected with hers. Lived it when, at last, he embraced her, joining in that ancient, fundamental way.

He understood now what it meant to love Ana, when she needed him more than ever.

HE SAW HER THROUGH THE WINDOW, HUDDLED OVER THE kitchen table, face pressed into the wood. Her kitty, Cocoa, cuddled near her face.

Ana lifted her head at the sound of Finn's knock, and her swollen, tear-stained face came into view. *Oh, Ana.*

"Please, I know what happened, and I only want to help," he pleaded, when she made no move toward the door. "Ana, it's Christmas."

"Go home, Finn," her cracked voice responded.

Finn drew in a breath and then called, "Ana, if I have to break this door down, I will!" An empty threat, they both knew it.

Ana made her way slowly to the door, pressing her forehead against the glass. He could now clearly see the bruise on her forehead, the gash in the center. He laid his own face against the spot opposite hers. "I'm begging you to go home. If you care about me at all, you'll leave. Please," she said.

Finn swallowed back the wave of emotions brewing inside, and slowly backed away. What else could he do? Ana wasn't begging to be rescued. She wasn't asking for comfort. Caring for her was accepting her, even when her needs were confusing and painful. If he loved her as much as he claimed he did, he'd acknowledge what she needed now was to be alone, no matter how much his heart cried out to comfort her.

Finn remembered his mother telling the story of how she met her husband, Andrew. He'd come into her father's pub, in Ireland, ordering a Guinness and a Shepherd's Pie. When she served it to him, a young girl of sixteen who'd never so much as kissed a boy, he knew right then and there that he'd marry her. He continued coming, day after day, for a week. Finally, he'd asked Claire's father for permission to marry her. They were married immediately. *Your father told me later, in one of his rare moments of sentimentality, he knew the moment he laid eyes on me. He didn't even like Shepherd's Pie. Sometimes, you just know, Finnegan. And we knew.*

*Sometimes you just know.*

# 11
## ANA

Ana had never before spent Christmas alone. Back home, the Deschanel clan was massive, every holiday a colossal fete. She never thought much about gatherings. She'd taken them for granted, as people often did with those things in life contributing to normalcy. She missed home now, as she sat alone on the antique couch, Cocoa curled up in her lap. She missed the sensation of knowing what to expect, from the smell of breakfast sausage in the *Ophélie* kitchens on an early Christmas morning, to the soft din of Catholic hymns; the hazy, mystical air underscoring the day. There was an honest magic about Christmas, but today, nothing felt magical.

Outside, a fresh snow came down, blanketing the earth once more. The only noise a ceaseless, dull churn as the ocean ebbed and flowed over the beach. The muted sensations provided a comfort to Ana, mirroring her own numb thoughts.

Not only was this Ana's first Christmas alone, it was her first where she had no contact of any kind with Nicolas. Her beloved cousin had been her dearest friend all her life. He'd been by her side at every critical moment, as well as all the inconsequential ones. There was no one else in the world she'd given so much of herself to. They loved each other, and perhaps it was a dangerous love, but how was she to know he would, eventually, take that closeness and attempt to step over the fine line protecting what they had? How could she have foreseen his love for her would turn to something more?

Maybe it was inevitable. They'd been dancing the dance for years. But it wasn't until Ana had a brief liaison with Oz that things escalated to a boiling point. Nicolas had never begrudged her any relationship, but this was different. Oz had, many years ago, been Ana's first love. That they'd rekindled it for an evening, years later, was a wound close enough to Nicolas' heart to push his feelings to the surface. Nicolas could neither change his thoughts nor act upon them. His hurt ran too deep.

Though she knew he wouldn't call, Ana couldn't help glancing toward the old phone on the wall, willing it to ring. All her calls and emails to him went unreturned, but a small part of her thought, *No, it's Christmas. Nicolas won't turn his back today of all days.* As the hours ticked by, her hurt grew to anger. *I've never needed you more than I do now. Never been this hurt, or afraid. Or lost. I don't deserve this.*

Finn had been by a number of times. First, the night before, he called to her through the door, obviously intoxicated. *Ana!* he'd cried. *I love you!*

Ana opened the door just a crack, long enough to see Finn's flushed, wild look. He pleaded with her to let him in so they could talk. Well, she didn't want to talk about what happened, but even if she had, she wouldn't do so with him in such a state. So she sent him home.

But he came back, every couple of hours, like clockwork, and now sober. Eventually, seeing his face was too painful, and she stopped answering his summons.

By Christmas morning, he was back at her door.

*Please, I want to help you,* Finn said calmly, through the glass pane. *Ana, it's Christmas.*

*Go home Finn.* Easier to reply without emotion than let it overcome her.

She loved him. There was no longer any use denying it. But Jon was right. He was a disgusting, horrible excuse for a man, but he was right. *Ana, you can never step away from what's inside you. And eventually you can't help sharing it with others.*

"*Oh come, oh come, Emmanuel, for Christ is born in Israel,*" Ana sang softly to Cocoa, as she stared out the window, at the crashing surf. Cocoa responded with low, persistent purrs and an affectionate kneading of paws against Ana's leg.

• • •

Ana awoke the next day around noon to the sound of someone at the door. Assuming Finn had returned, she hastily wrapped her robe around her, and, with a sigh now growing too familiar, went to send him away again.

But when she pushed the small, white curtain aside, it wasn't Finn staring back at her. It was her Aunt Colleen, from New Orleans, carrying a small, black valise, and dressed as if she were meeting the president for brunch.

Ana flung the door open, and her aunt's lavender perfume filled her senses, rendering her full of nostalgia and a number of other welcome, familiar emotions. "My darling," Colleen exclaimed, resting her luggage against the mat, leaning in to embrace her niece. "New Orleans is not the same in your absence!"

Ana picked up her aunt's luggage, and ushered her inside. "What are you doing here?"

"Amelia," Colleen replied, as if it were explanation enough. Amelia was Colleen's daughter, and an empath. Her keen senses were among the strongest in the entire family. "Dear, please tell me you have some nice, strong coffee in this old house?"

"I'll make some," Ana said distantly, wondering for a moment if she was sleeping, and dreaming of home.

Ana adored her Aunt Colleen, one of her father's sisters, and was close to her in a way she wasn't close with most of her relatives. Colleen shouldered the responsibility of keeping the family together, and considered herself the head of affairs for all Deschanels, and was, in a more formal sense, the head of their magical needs, being the magistrate of the Deschanel Magi Collective. She had a knack for assessing the family's needs and promptly taking steps to address issues. Years ago, that included, along with her other sister, Elizabeth, taking a young, motherless Ana under her wing to ensure she had a proper female role model. Though Ana's father remarried, Ana had never been especially close with Barbara. Colleen and Elizabeth were both surrogate mothers, then and now.

Colleen was also a healer, though Colleen's powers were of a broader scope than Ana's. Unlike Ana, Colleen could heal others. She'd spent her life doing it, letting her magical healing cross over into the scientific as she pursued a life in medicine.

Ana felt a light pressure on the back of her head where Colleen planted a firm, comforting kiss. "My dear," Colleen began, "I fear Amelia was right. Darling, what happened to your face?"

Ana felt the long overdue tears threatening under her lids. *No, don't do it. If you start, you'll never stop.* If she turned and witnessed the gentle compassion in her aunt's face, she might dissolve entirely. "Yes," she said, still facing the coffee pot, avoiding the question about her injury, "Amelia was right."

Colleen's hands massaged Ana's upper arms, and

then she broke away, taking a seat at the kitchen table. "I hope you don't see it as an intrusion. Amelia, as with all those who sometimes sense trouble in the family, meant well, I assure you. She loves you, Ana. You cousins were close, once upon a time, until you and Nicolas broke off into your own world. She had one of her intuitions two days ago, and I booked the first flight out this morning."

Ana poured her aunt some coffee, with shaking hands. The glass carafe trembled against the ceramic mug, and she stopped, steadying herself. The smell of coffee, something she normally loved, was nauseating. "I love Amelia, too. She has a good heart, just like her mother," she reassured her aunt. Ana turned toward her aunt, accepting the mug. "But you really didn't have to come all the way out here, Aunt C. Wouldn't a phone call have been easier?"

Colleen took a long, deep sip of the coffee, sighed, and set the mug down. Her manicured nails were a perfectly respectable shade of mauve. "Which would've accomplished nothing, knowing how private you are. I really am ashamed of my brother for leaving you out here on your own, so separated from all of us. And where's Nicolas in all this?" she asked with a light *tsk,* rapping her nails on the table.

"I'm thirty years old," Ana reminded her aunt, as she took a seat. "My father didn't leave me. I chose to come here."

Colleen tilted her head to the right, studying her niece carefully. “And what of Nicolas?”

“That’s a long story,” Ana said, letting her breath out slowly.

Her aunt slipped one arm over the back of the chair, and crossed her slender legs. “Better start talking then. Begin with the bruise on your forehead.”

Before her aunt arrived, Ana had no desire to talk, or even think, about all that happened. But something about Colleen’s presence soothed her immensely, and the words began to flow freely. *Healers and empaths. No such thing as not wanting to talk about it in this family,* she thought, with bitter humor.

Instead of leading with her injury, she began where the problem started: that foolish night in New Orleans, with Oz. How Oz’s guilt ate at him even more than Ana’s had, how she’d left home for his sake, coming to Maine to try and put it behind her. She spoke of her chilly reception by the islanders, with Jon being the rudest of all. How Finn’s kind and warm words contrasted with all of it, providing a very unexpected comfort.

Then, Nicolas and Oz came to Maine, and Oz subsequently poured out his guilty conscience, confessing to his best friend what he had done. Ana would never forget the censure in Nicolas’ eyes as he pummeled her with judgment, assuring her he would never again be a part of her life.

And then, Jon.

"Nicolas isn't talking to me. Finn wants to talk, but I have no words for him. My head is throbbing, and all I want to do is walk straight into the Atlantic and keep going," Ana finished, realizing her words were true.

"That is quite a conundrum," Colleen agreed, gazing out the window, thoughtfully. "Have you considered calling the police?"

"The police?" Ana repeated, taken aback.

Colleen leaned forward, choosing her words carefully. "Ana, what Jon did to you was assault. It isn't okay."

Ana balked at this, looking away. "He's Finn's brother. I can't do that."

"You *can*," Colleen disagreed firmly.

Ana diverted her gaze. "I'm not... I'm sorry, but I can't think about that right now."

"I won't push you to do something you're not comfortable with, or ready for." Her aunt paused. "Tell me, Ana, why won't you talk to Finn? Do you not believe him, when he says he wants to help you?"

"I believe him," Ana said slowly, finding her words. "Finn's a good man. Honorable. He deserves a good woman."

"You're a spectacular woman," Colleen argued. "One of my utmost favorites, in fact." Cocoa chose this moment to join the ladies in conversation, jumping onto a chair next to Aunt Colleen and purring enthusiastically in agreement with their guest. Colleen offered an affectionate scratch behind Cocoa's ear.

Ana returned her thoughts to her aunt's question. "You have to say that. And I love you for it, but I'm tired of being the cause of pain in others. Nicolas, Oz, Finn. The common denominator here is me."

Colleen finished her coffee, dropping her arms on to the table. "Anasofiya Aleksandrovna. You know damn well Oz is a grown man, responsible for his own actions. And yes, your darling Finn is hurting, but only because of what his own brother did to you!" Colleen's eyes narrowed, her thin brows furrowing, as she added, "And Nicolas is your *cousin*. Everyone in this family knows that boy loves you, just as surely as we know he can't help it. But he chose to act like a buffoon, and punish you when he had no business doing so. You didn't deserve that, nor did you cause it."

Colleen's wisdom was lost on Ana, who had already deliberated and meted judgment upon herself. "I wish... sometimes I think..." Ana didn't know how to say the words. They'd plagued her heart for so many years, but something about voicing them felt more painful than the longing itself. "I wish my mother was here. She was a good woman, and if she hadn't died, maybe I'd be more like her."

Colleen took on the look of a mother hen, ruffled feathers and all. "You believe that, do you?"

Ana nodded.

"Well," Colleen continued, settling back into her chair in a dramatic fashion, as if indicating they better get comfortable. "Then I have a story to tell you. I never intended to, because it isn't my story to tell, but I see now there isn't a way around it."

"I don't understand."

Colleen drew in a deep, dignified breath, letting it out slowly. "My dear, it is time to tell you about your mother."

# 12
## COLLEEN

*I suppose you know the basics already: your mother, Ekatherina, fled Russia for the United States as an au pair, hoping to make enough money to bring her parents and siblings over. She changed her name to Catherine, managed to get into business school, and through a favor, obtained a role in the finance department at Deschanel Media Group. Back then, of course, your father was very young and suffered from an overly focused, incurable entrepreneurial spirit. Though my brother was often an intense young man who wasn't prone to sentiment of any kind, he almost immediately fell in love with your mother. He told me, once, he saw the same determination in her as he felt in his own ambitions, and greatly admired her courage in leaving everything she cared about behind for a chance at a better life. He related to that, having been determined to build something more than what he'd inherited.*

*Your father married Catherine, hoping to help her*

*family immigrate to the United States. But Augustus' confidence of youth led him to believe it was as simple as waving around the Deschanel credit card. Immigration during the Communist era was challenging, and the process got wrapped up in layer upon layer of bureaucracy, as the tension between the countries ebbed and flowed. Augustus worked tirelessly at the matter, but it became clear they would need to be patient. Catherine, who's vocabulary did not include that word in any form, began growing resentful of your father.*

*I don't believe she wed him simply for his ability to help her, but I've always suspected she didn't marry him entirely out of love, either. Your aunt Evangeline was suspicious from the start, and it drove a wedge between your father and her for a while. I don't know if he ever told you this, but Evangeline was with your father from the very start, before Deschanel Media even had carpet, or functioning plumbing. She put off college to help him, after your aunt Madeline died, and your father threw himself into work to nurse his broken heart.*

*You know your father's ability. His gift of persuasion is legend. Augustus could convince the happiest man alive to jump off the Crescent City Connection. As a boy, the ability often reared to the surface even when he wasn't trying, though he loathed it, and resented us the few times we asked him to use it for the good of the family. I believe Augustus wanted her so badly, he couldn't help influencing her decision subliminally.*

*Sensing his wife's growing disquiet, your father knew he*

*must seek to find ways of keeping her happy or risk losing her. Augustus, a man who didn't believe in taking days off, was suddenly planning vacations with his wife, trying to find even one place that might inspire her. Though he wanted to take her back home, travel to the USSR in her situation was precarious at best. So home was out of the question, leaving him unable to take her to the one place she really wanted to go.*

*It was an old associate who told your father about the small islands off the coast of Maine. They were the closest location in the country to western Russia, in both geography and climate. Your father—again, not a man of whimsy—thought perhaps a retreat home in Maine might help her feel closer to her family.*

*But Augustus didn't know his wife the way he thought he did.*

*When they arrived on Summer Island to take ownership of the property, your parents were treated like royalty. In a way, they were. The community had long been ignored by the wider world, and your father buying a house on their quant little island was the most excitement they'd had in many years. Maybe ever.*

*Mayor Cairne, whose son is now the current mayor, spent a considerable amount of time showing them around, and getting to know the young couple. I don't know whether the attraction was immediate between George and Catherine, but at some point in the two weeks they spent on the island, a very dangerous chemistry developed.*

*Your father was completely oblivious to it. Love must*

*truly be blind, because your father has never been one to miss a detail.*

*But he missed it entirely during the many hours they spent dining at the Cairne's home, or off touring the island and mainland. Nor did he catch on when, upon the end of their trip, Catherine cheerfully insisted she would stay a little longer, on her own.*

*Augustus left her here, confused at her decision, but also relieved that she seemed restored of her good nature. Your father has a habit, as you know, of closing the book on a problem and moving swiftly to the next issue. He did so with this, although I don't think he deserves any blame in what happened next.*

*While he may have been blind to what was going on with his wife, the community of Summer Island was not. Everyone had seen the sidelong glances between Catherine and the very married George Cairne, and those who had not, quickly heard about it. You know how rumors spread. First, with a glimmer of truth, and later, with shocking embellishments. Soon, people were claiming to have seen them going at it in the town square.*

*The damage was done. You can keep an old behavior under wraps well enough, but new love is especially difficult to hide completely. By the time rumors claimed a full-on affair, that was exactly what was happening.*

*Catherine's extended stay began as a week and stretched into months. I believe she would've stayed forever, she was so in love with George, had it not been for the utterly awful way the islanders treated her.*

*We all know it takes two. But George and his wife were much beloved members of the community, the Cairnes having been on the island since the town was formally established. Catherine Deschanel was an interloper, and a foreigner, at that. They didn't hesitate to brand her all sorts of terrible names, accusing her of corrupting the man and ruining his family. The essence of celebrity eroded, and people rued the day Deschanels stepped foot on their island. Ultimately, George himself asking her to leave finally pushed her to return home.*

*Your mother returned home heartbroken at the defection of a man who promised he would leave his wife, and make a new life with her. Not too long after, she learned she was pregnant, and Catherine was understandably terrified Augustus would realize she was carrying a love child, and cast her out. Or worse, send her back to the USSR.*

*Before you worry yourself too much, dear, you are absolutely, one hundred percent, the daughter of Augustus Deschanel. You are the spitting image of your grandmother, my mother Colleen, and you strongly resemble so many other Deschanels. That you are a healer is further proof. The date of your conception was a month or more after she came back to New Orleans, in any case. But your mother didn't know this. Her intimacy with your father, and George, was timed so closely together that she couldn't be sure. Not knowing drove her mad.*

*I know your father never told you this next part, and it was to protect you, as I am sure you'll understand and forgive. Your mother tried, numerous times, to terminate the pregnancy. Throwing herself down the stairs, swallowing poisonous things. She stopped eating, refusing to care for herself at all. Your aunt Elizabeth, not even eighteen yet, moved in and looked after her full time, they were so scared of what she might do.*

*Your father pleaded with her to think of you, to fight the melancholia, but there was no getting through to her. She didn't want your father's child, and having George's would be a disaster. Her life was in shambles. It was a wonder the pregnancy made it to term. In hindsight, perhaps your healing abilities protected you even in utero.*

*Your father called your Aunt Evangeline and me. Augustus resented being asked to use his, so was reluctant to ask us to use ours. But when he found himself in dire need, he had no one else to turn to.*

*In the end, we couldn't heal her, because she bore no physical afflictions.*

*Sadly, your mother died within days of giving birth to you. The doctors believed it was a result of the injuries she sustained while torturing herself. The truth is, no one knows. And sometimes, even with modern medicine what it is, women still die of childbirth complications.*

*Why have I told you this story, my dear? Surely you must be wondering why I'd risk causing you further pain when you're already suffering so. It's simple. It's not pain I'm hoping this story gives you. My goal is clarity. Truth. And the freedom found only in both.*

*It is quite lovely to idolize one's mother. Daughters have a way of forgiving their mother's faults, as I am sure, one day, you will forgive yours. But when that idolization leads to self-abandonment, as it has with you... well, I can't let that happen. I will not watch you punish yourself for not being more like your mother, when your mother was a flawed individual, like all of us.*

*Ana, you are who you are, and there's nothing, not a single thing, wrong with that. You have the introspective intelligence of your father, the kind heart of your grandmother, the selflessness of your grandfather, August. You needn't put anyone on a false pedestal.*

*You are who you are, and that's exactly who you should be.*

THROUGHOUT THE TELLING OF HER STORY, COLLEEN OBSERVED Ana's expression evolve from curiosity to anger, to a confused hurt. It was a gamble, sharing this story of her mother. Some would argue, even, a cruelty to shatter the image Ana held of a mother she couldn't remember. But Colleen felt it an even greater injustice to allow Ana to continue her cycle of self-punishment while she sought to attain the approval of a person who had never existed.

"Now I know why everyone on the island was so cold to me," Ana said after a long, painful pause. "They see me, and they see my mother."

"I suspect you're correct," Colleen confirmed. "Though I think you've quite won them over with your lighthouse restoration project. I would tell you that was a brilliant move, but I know you didn't do it to win hearts."

"No," Ana agreed, "I didn't."

Ana still hadn't commented directly on anything Colleen revealed. This alarmed her, as she was well aware of her niece's tendency to retreat back into herself, and shut down emotionally.

"I can't read your mind, dear. You're blocking, as well you should be. But this means you'll need to tell me what you're thinking," Colleen said finally.

Ana pulled her hair back off her face, and Colleen saw, for the first time, beyond the strangely unhealed physical wounds, just how tired her niece looked. Her pale skin had a sallow appearance, the dark, black circles under her eyes a startling juxtaposition. "I'm just like her, aren't I?"

Colleen was taken aback. "No, darling, you are *nothing* like her." This was not what she'd hoped for, in telling this story. Ana was supposed to feel soothed, and free of the bonds tethering her to this false belief. "Your mother had no remorse whatsoever for how she treated your father. Or you."

"But she hurt everyone she touched. My father. George's family. This entire community. Me. Intentions don't matter when the results are so catastrophic."

"Of course intentions matter," Colleen corrected, wrapping her long fingers around Ana's wrist. "Everyone makes mistakes. Every single person who has ever walked this great planet has regrets. Your mother's only regret was that her plans to run away with George Cairne were thwarted. She didn't care one lick about how her actions affected anyone else."

Ana politely withdrew her wrist, then stood, wrapping her robe tight around her. "I know it wasn't easy to tell me all that. And I know you're here because you love me, and are worried. I love you too," she said, folding herself against the wall. "You've always been so good to me, and I don't even know how to express how much it means that you cared enough to come check on my well-being."

"Ana—"

"But now I know it's not just me. It's in my blood."

"There's simply no such thing as genetic selfishness, dear. It's a learned behavior," Colleen insisted. She knew she was losing Ana. Her niece may have inherited her mother's melancholia, but she had her father's single-minded stubbornness.

"I can't escape who I am," Ana countered. "I've tried my whole life to fight it. To be normal, and force myself to connect with others. The only person it's ever worked with is Nicolas, and where did that get me? He'll never speak to me again, because I've managed to hurt him, too."

"It's preposterous you continue to blame yourself for his emotive mood swings! Dear, he has no business—"

Ana shook her head. "I knew how he felt about me. I've always known. And I knew what happened with Oz would hurt him, and I did it anyway. Maybe I wanted him to find out; to hurt him. To force him to leave."

"You really are as pig-headed as your father!"

Ana dropped her head, as deep, rasping breaths consumed her. "It all hurts so much."

Colleen stepped forward and pulled her niece into her arms, a warm embrace intended to express what words evidently could not. Ana attempted to twist free, but Colleen held tighter, until she felt Ana's tension dissolve. Her niece's struggles slowly turned to sobs.

"There now, darling," Colleen whispered, kissing the top of Ana's head. "It's been a long day, and you're overwhelmed. You've not even focused enough to heal your wounds. Let's get you into bed, and we can talk more tomorrow."

Ana nodded, and let her aunt guide her to the bedroom, even obediently taking the valium Colleen offered.

Ana's guard dropped, and Colleen saw her niece's mind laid bare as she tenderly tucked her beneath the covers. Ana, for the first time, wasn't yearning for her mother's warmth. She was sufficiently comforted by the woman who *had* always been there for her, by choice, even now, when she believed herself to be completely alone in the world.

Colleen lay her lips against her niece's forehead, careful to avoid the ragged cut, as Ana settled into her bed. "Rest child. Tomorrow will feel so much better."

# 13
# ANA

Ana found Aunt Colleen in the kitchen with her bags packed. The older woman patiently sipped her coffee, reading the Summer Island Gazette.

"How are you this morning, darling?" Colleen asked, looking up.

"Tired," Ana murmured, running a hand through her messy hair. "I feel hung-over."

"Emotional catharsis will have that effect," Colleen said knowingly. "Of course, the valium might be a factor as well." She folded the paper carefully, tucking it under her placemat. "I'm sorry to make this visit so short. The hospital needs me, as always."

"It means a lot to me that you came," Ana said. When her eyes first opened, the events of the prior night seemed surreal, as if they'd happened in a lucid dream.

Now, with the day behind her, everything began to sink in. She was weighted by her conclusions.

"I'm never more than a call away, my dear," Colleen said. "Sometimes it helps to be reminded you're not as alone as you might believe."

Grateful more than ever for her aunt's unconditional love, Ana hesitantly inquired, "Would you mind if I asked one more favor of you?"

"Anything I can do to help, darling. What is it you need?"

"There are still more questions than answers right now. I don't know what the future holds. Cocoa is a good cat, and has been a huge comfort to me. It would help me to know that, whatever I decide, she's cared for." Ana added, in a final rush, "Would you take her home with you? To The Gardens?"

Aunt Colleen gave her a considering look. Careful to guard her darkest thoughts, Ana allowed her some access.

Soft of heart for all living creatures, Colleen agreed.

Within the hour, Colleen and Cocoa were gone, and Ana had the house to herself again.

Wrapping herself in a thick robe, she ventured back to the porch. The late December morning air hit her like a wave of ice, but there was something almost soothing about this shock to her system. The salt and sea foam rose up to greet her, and she welcomed the assault on her senses.

Ana had a sudden urge to cast off her robe and

wander down into the cool sand until she hit the shoreline. She imagined the sensation of the icy ocean lapping at her toes, then ankles, as she ventured further into the water until there was nothing left except her dull, distant heartbeat. The memories of all she'd done, erased. Carried away with the tide.

Instead, she sunk into the wicker rocker and closed her eyes, letting her toes move the chair back and forth, slowly.

Ana didn't realize she'd dozed off until she felt a shadow pass before her, accompanied by the sensation she was no longer alone.

Opening her eyes, she saw Finn standing awkwardly on her porch, hands buried deep in his pockets. He looked as exhausted and worn down as she felt. *As Aunt Colleen said, I've not even focused long enough to heal my own wounds.*

"Can we please talk?" he asked. It wasn't quite begging, but was close enough that Ana felt a twinge of guilt at how she'd ignored him the past few days.

She nodded, resigned, and moved back into the house, as Finn followed.

Nervously, she poured herself a cup of tea as he sat down at the table behind her. Still not quite ready to talk, Ana made him a mug as well, but it wasn't until he said, "Ana, sit down, sweetie," that she finally did.

Ana looked down at the mug wedged between her palms, avoiding eye contact. Finn reached a hand across the table, but then pulled it back, and this only made her heart race harder.

"Ana," he whispered, stretching his hand again, this time toward her face. He stopped just shy of touching her. "My god, I am so sorry. I didn't realize what was happening, and I didn't mean what I said. I am so unbelievably sorry."

She didn't know how to acknowledge this. His own brother had done it, and she, somehow, had allowed it to get that far. She wasn't foolish enough to believe she'd caused Jon's attack, but in a roundabout way her being there created this situation; this rift.

"Tell me what to do to help you," Finn said. His words were careful, but the cracks in his voice were real. "Anything, Ana, and I'll do it."

Before she could speak, her eyes caught sight of his purple, swollen knuckles. "Your hand," she said, gently running the tips of her fingers over the distended joints of his right hand. "What happened?"

"Jon," Finn replied, a touch embarrassed. "It's fine, really."

It wasn't fine. His hand was at the very least fractured, and likely broken. She could fix it. She knew this now, that her power extended to Finn, too. But it wasn't the time to tell Finn who she was.

"I never want to talk about the details of Christmas Eve," Ana replied, answering his earlier question. There was nothing to be gained from it, and to relive it would not only be horrible for her, but would drive a wedge further between the brothers. "Not ever."

"We don't have to," he said gently. She watched as his eyes couldn't help but be drawn to the bruise on her face, how he flinched each time. "I'll kill him," he added, almost to himself.

"No," Ana corrected. "He's your brother. You need to make peace with him."

"We're past that being an option," Finn said, the hardness in his voice suggesting there was no use arguing him on the point. "All I want to do right now is take you far away from here. I wish I could go back a week, and do exactly that, so this never would've happened."

Ana realized, with sinking dread, Finn blamed himself. "I'm honestly fine," she lied.

He looked down at his hands in nervous contemplation. "I almost did kill him. I wanted to. I was blinded with the rage I felt for him, even as I saw him lying there, helpless, not fighting back." Finn raised his hands before him, looking over the swollen knots. "But something stopped me. Inside of me, for the first time in my life, a voice told me to just... let it go." He dropped his hands and looked up, and in his eyes she saw a look more serious than anyone had ever given her before. "That voice was yours, Ana."

Ana slipped a hand over his uninjured one, and gave a gentle squeeze. This was no small revelation for Finn. "I'm glad you stopped. And I'm sure Jon is at home right now having some realizations of his own. He's your brother, so there has to be some good in him, somewhere."

"I can't figure out, for the life of me, why you're defending him. Do you—" Finn's question ended there, but Ana understood, instinctively, what he left unsaid: *do you have feelings for him?*

"I detest him," Ana replied succinctly. "But I can't help feeling like this could've been avoided if I'd just left after all that stuff with Alex."

"Ana—" he started, then stopped, evidently realizing he couldn't argue with her when she was feeling like this. He watched her for several long moments, and then finally asked, "Do you have genuine feelings for me?"

Ana paused. If she said it, it would be harder to walk away. If she didn't, she'd be lying. *Lies have only hurt the people you love.*

"I love you," she said.

Finn dropped his gaze, but the relief on his face was palpable. She never realized the man had any insecurities until then. In a rush, he forged ahead, "Then never say things like that. Please, never say silly things about leaving, or about hurting me. And get it out of your head that I'm somehow *mad* at you for what happened with you and Jon back in November. It hurts a little, knowing you were... with him, like that. It hurts more than I'd like to admit, but I can get over it. I already have." He pushed his mug aside, and bowed his face over his folded hands. "What hurts more is that you kept it from me, because of some ridiculous need to protect me. For future reference, never, ever feel like you need to do that with me, Ana. I'll never punish you for the truth. Okay?"

Ana nodded, but said nothing, waiting for him to go on.

"But what Jon did to you, I can't forgive it," he continued. His face and neck blossomed with red. "And worse, I saw how he'd been treating you, these past months, and did nothing. I thought he was mad at me, for finding someone, or maybe jealous. I never in all my wildest nightmares imagined this. That he would hurt you. I feel as though I've never known him."

"You couldn't have foreseen something like that," Ana said. He was condemning his brother, whom he had known his whole life, in favor of her, a girl Jon had referred to as Finn's *most recent amusement*. "And if I'd just left, maybe he could've dealt with things better."

"Left?" Finn shook his head, looking as if he wanted to hug her and shake her all at once. "Do you have any idea how much it hurts me when you say things like that? You don't deserve me? You're just going to hurt me? I'm tired of hearing it, Ana, because it isn't true! And you really aren't giving me enough credit for being able to put my big boy pants on and deal with things."

"Okay," Ana conceded, "but you did get hurt."

"No, my eyes were opened," he gently corrected. "I know I can be a hothead. I act first, and think later, because it takes me a while to process things. But now I know. I know everything I need to know, and I'm not hurt. I'm horrified."

"I'm not excusing Jon's actions," Ana replied, "but he is your brother—"

"My *brother* would never do that to me, or to someone I love," Finn interrupted, clenching his jaw. "My *brother* would get over it, for my sake. My *brother* wouldn't try to force himself on my girlfriend. He'd never cause her physical harm." With this, his eyes fell on her forehead again, wincing. "He would *get over it.*"

Ana dropped her eyes. "I'm not that unlike him, Finn."

When Finn looked up, the anger had drained away and what remained was a glimpse of the love she'd seen on the cliffs. It felt like forever ago. "I know you, Anasofiya Aleksandrovna Vasilyeva Deschanel," he said. "I know you like my own heart."

"You don't know the dark things in my heart Finn," she replied. "There's poison there, and it'll poison you, too."

He smiled sadly. "For such an intelligent woman, you say the oddest things. Your heart is dark from your own sadness, Ana. From not allowing yourself the happiness you deserve. I can give it to you, and do you know why?"

"I don't," she admitted.

"Because I know you. I know who you are, and I don't want you to change. I absolutely forbid it."

"You're telling me it's okay for me to be like this, but

not Jon? You're condemning him for the same things you're trying to encourage in me."

"Ana," Finn leaned forward, this time taking her folded hands in his. "You're filled with remorse and the desire to be good. To do good. Jon does as he wants, with zero regard for who he hurts in the process. It took me years to finally see him for who he is. He won't change."

"Neither will I."

"You don't need to. You're perfect just the way you are."

His acceptance of her only made Ana feel worse. He was blinding himself to the same things he had, for years, blinded himself toward his brother. He attached a goodness to her she didn't deserve, being intentionally short-sighted as to who she was, without seeing the irony in the comparison.

"Marry me," he blurted out, so quickly and unexpectedly her head spun as if slapped.

"What?"

"That didn't come out as smoothly as I'd hoped," he said, frowning. Then he dropped down on one knee before her, slipping from his pocket a small blue velvet box. It was old, and inside, Ana knew even before seeing, was his mother's ring. "I love you. I wish I hadn't said all the reasons why a minute ago because they were all the things I wanted to say right now."

"We... Finn, we barely know each other."

"Remember the story of my how my mother and

father met?" He didn't wait for her acknowledgement. "My father knew the moment he met her. Two weeks later, they were married. *Sometimes you know*, my mother told me. And I know."

Ana had a dozen rational refusals to toss back at him, but the truth was, she knew, too. She had never, not once, been in love like this before. It was so foreign to her that she'd tried to disregard the creeping realization, but denying it changed nothing. Her love for Finn was more powerful than anything she'd ever experienced, and it happened before she could protect either of them from it. The impracticality of it didn't make it less real, and her defense of them barely knowing one another was weak. They knew each other better than she knew people she'd known her entire life. Their bond had formed swiftly, and strongly.

"Ana, I'm not expecting you to give me a firm yes. I know you weren't expecting this," he ventured cautiously.

Now that the objections had passed, she was left with her own, raw feelings about it. *Finn. Love. Marriage.* With a terrible, sinking sensation, she realized she wanted all three.

"Okay," she whispered, voice hoarse. Looking up then, she drew in a deep, joyous breath and said again, somewhat louder, "Okay."

"Doesn't have to be right away. I can wait," Finn reassured, sensing her hesitant fear. He slipped the ring over her finger, then pressed his lips over the top. It fit perfectly. "I don't want you to think I'm pressuring you. I never want you to feel cornered, or like I want you to do or be anything other than who you are."

"It isn't that," Ana insisted. "A lot has happened in the past week, and this feels really..."

"Desperate? Sudden?" She laughed at his mind reading. "Shit, I know. That's what I'd think, too. I've never been in love before, but this is how I know my feelings now. Because if you were anyone else, I'd let you walk away, and I'd never look back."

"Actually, I understand perfectly," she replied. And she did.

THE DISCUSSION CONTINUED ON, BUT ANA REMEMBERED little except Finn eventually drawing her into his arms, and into her bed. She recalled with perfect clarity the way his hands felt across her skin, like safety and sensuality. How Finn insisted on taking it slower than the day on the cliff, instead tracing his lips over every inch, every contour of her body.

Her heart would also never forget the way his muscles trembled under her hands as he took her slowly, rhythmically, controlling his motions so as not to finish too soon. How the slight stubble on his chin brushed across her forehead, and her breasts, as his kisses landed with each stroke of his lovemaking.

Finn loved her with impressive self-control, and as she allowed him his release and reward, he recovered quickly. Soon morning turned to afternoon, then afternoon to evening. Before slipping off to sleep, he whispered, against her collarbone, “Ana, you’re the first safe place I’ve ever had.”

Cutting off any need for a response, her mighty Poseidon was almost immediately snoring softly at her breast. “I feel exactly the same about you,” she whispered anyway, laying a kiss atop his head.

For so long, so many years, she believed Nicolas was her safe place. But his safety was a false economy, instead only shielding her from a world she’d have to face eventually. What Finn gave her, and what she now knew she gave him, was so much more. It was real. a two-way mirror reflecting at each other the good, the bad, and everything in between.

Whatever lay between them had grown over the past hours. But as that love grew, so did Ana’s fears, and, along with them, the growing sense she could not, and should not, continue to draw this out. They were already nearing the point of no return.

No, they’d passed it, tonight.

Knowing Finn could sleep through anything, Ana tenderly placed both hands over his injured one, sending her focused energies through to him, healing him. The purple slowly faded, the swelling eased.

Ana then mended her own wounds.

*Love,* she thought, as she drifted off. *That’s why I can heal him, when I’ve never been able to heal another before.*

*Love.*

# 14
## JON

Several days went by, and Finn hadn't been home, not even returning for a change of clothes. Jon didn't know if twenty-seven years of brotherhood would go out in a blaze of rage, or simply die a slow death, but the waiting was worse than the knowing.

Then Ana showed up at the veterinary office, early one morning. After she calmly requested to talk, he locked the door, and ushered her to the back, before he could deduce what her intentions might be.

Ana sat across from him. *Did she come here to remind me? To rub it in?*

"If you're looking for an apology—"

"Stop," Ana interrupted, putting a hand in front of her, her manner suggesting it was more than a request. It was a warning; a barrier. "Even if you gave me one, you wouldn't mean it and neither of us would feel better. That isn't why I'm here."

"Why, then, are you here?" Jon asked, narrowing his eyes in suspicion. He wondered, briefly, if Finn was outside waiting for a cue to come in and jump him.

"For Finn," Ana replied, folding her hands across her lap. "No matter what passed between you and I, you're brothers. I don't want to be what comes between your relationship."

"Too late for that," Jon muttered, not bothering to reassure her of the fallacy in her statement. It was good she believed it. If she believed it enough, she might yet leave. Things might repair themselves.

Ana drew in a deep breath, her eyes momentarily fluttering closed. "You're an asshole, Jon. You really are. But I can try to look past it, for Finn's sake. It doesn't have to be this way."

"You know it does," Jon replied. It wasn't a lie. He was incapable of adjusting to any future that included her. He couldn't "look past it for Finn's sake," nor did he much care if that made him childish.

Before she could respond, Jon's eyes caught the glint of something sparkling on her hand. A ring. "What... my mother's ring... he *gave you my mother's ring?"*

"Not that it matters to me what you think about it," Ana began, without even a hint of apology, drawing her shoulders back. "But yes. It's why I'm trying to help the two of you make amends."

"You're just like your mother," Jon hissed, standing

up so fast his metal chair thumped off the plaster wall. “You couldn’t resist coming here, like she did, and messing up everyone’s lives!”

Ana looked stricken by the comment. “Go ahead Jon, project your shit on me. I can take it. I’m—”

“That blue dress,” Jon cut in. “That *whore’s* dress. Did you wonder, Ana, why everyone couldn’t stop staring at you at that ridiculous lighthouse event? Why people were whispering? Because your mother wore that dress when she seduced George Cairne and ruined his marriage! Everyone knows the story!”

“Jon—”

“*I hate you*!” Jon screamed, the sharp sound resonating across the sparse office. “I hate you, Ana! I hate everything about you! I hate the way you look at Finn, the way you walk across a room, the way you felt in my arms! I hate that stupid way you chew on your lower lip, and how you sleep with your mouth slightly parted! I hate the innocent, wide-eyed look you’re giving me now! And I’m *not sorry for what I did to you!* My only regret was Finn coming in before I could finish, and drive you away from here!”

Ana’s mouth hung in shocked silence, both trembling hands raised in surrender. “You’re a sociopath,” she said, losing her voice. “I’m going to take Finn far away from you, so you can never hurt him, or me, ever again.”

# 15
## ANA

A week passed. Despite Ana's resolve to forget Jon's cruel words, they stayed with her, haunting her. She'd lose herself in the ugly sentiment, but then Finn would flash her a smile, or brush a kiss against the back of her neck, and she'd tell herself, *we only need each other.*

But she couldn't ignore what the rift had done to Finn. With their parents gone, and no other family to speak of, he and Jon had relied on each other for so many years. Jon's words repeatedly came back to her, and her confidence faded to the old way of thinking. *Ana, you can never step away from what's inside you. And eventually you can't help sharing it with others, either.*

The situation escalated further when, following a fresh storm, a pine tree crashed through the roof of her house. Finn helped her secure a tarp over most of the exposed area, but it would be several days before anyone from Portland could come out to remove the tree and start repairs. This put them back at the St. Andrews house, and their presence birthed a molasses-thick hostility that grew and festered with every moment the three of them were forced to co-exist.

Several times, the unspoken words living in the silence nearly erupted, but Ana stayed Finn's hand with promises of their future.

For the most part, Jon confined his venom to her alone. One day, when he came upon her clearing away Christmas decorations, he slammed the star into a box, shattering it. From that moment on, she made a point of staying in their room when Finn wasn't home.

The environment was toxic to Ana, inadvertently from all sides. The deeper Finn wore his pain, the greater her own guilt blossomed. What Jon had done to her was unforgivable. But this suspended animation she and Finn lived in now was equally wrong. Her arrival on the island had driven a wedge between the brothers that might never mend. No matter what she did to focus on the positive, self-doubt always hung on the end, reminding her. *Darkness. Eventually you can't help sharing it with others.*

Then Oz called from New Orleans. *Nicolas needs you,* he said. *He's gotten himself into some trouble. With a girl.*

*I'm the last person Nicolas wants to see.*

*Maybe, but you're the person he needs.* Pause. *And I can't stay.*

Nicolas needed her. This was the catalyst required

to sway her into action. Oz even checked flights for her, and there was one very early the next morning. She could be home, in New Orleans, by tomorrow night.

Ana looked down at a sleeping Finn, and her heart swelled with painful love. *Real love. The first safe place I've ever known.*

But love was more than the connection of two hearts. It was more than passion forged in the melding of bodies. Love was about doing the right thing, and putting the other person's needs ahead of your own. It was about repairing a hurt by cutting off the source of the wound.

*This is the most difficult decision I've ever had to make.*

Ana set the diamond ring on the nightstand. Finn's soft snoring ceased, and Ana froze, fearful he might wake. Instead, he smiled in his sleep, and turned over, returning to his dreams.

"I'm so sorry," Ana whispered. She reached a hand out to touch him one last time, but pulled it back. No point in making this harder than it already was. "I really do love you, Finnegan James."

Ana tiptoed into the hall, resisting the urge to turn back and take him in one last time. She knelt, picking up her duffle bag, and continued with light steps down the hall, past Jon's room.

Ana loathed confrontation, but the urge to launch a barrage of assaults against Jon was almost too tempting to pass up. *You're wrong*, she would've said. *You and I are nothing alike. You're cruel, and have no qualms about bringing others down into your despair. We are both pariahs, but I, at least, refuse to continue to hurt people I love.*

But she wouldn't say that, or the thousand other things burning in the dark corners of her heart. Waking Jon meant waking Finn, and it would be easier to close both chapters at once. They'd both hate her, for different reasons. She couldn't care less what Jon thought of her, but Finn's inevitable confusion tore her heart in half. She'd have to find comfort in knowing he would be better off, in the end.

Angus padded toward her as she reached the front door. Finn told her once that Angus had never taken to anyone the way he took to Ana.

"Goodbye, little friend," Ana said, kneeling to allow Angus' relentless kisses. She scratched behind his ears, allowing herself one final, small distraction before walking away. "Take care of your master."

Ana left, looking back once more at the old Victorian as she trudged through the snowy driveway. The best, and the worst, memories of her life had happened here. And now, Nicolas needed her. She didn't know if he even knew she was coming, but she had to at least try to make things right. If she couldn't mend the situation here, perhaps she could at home.

Ten minutes later, Ana parked her father's car at the ferry docks. At the dark hour, there were only a handful of other passengers waiting to embark. The fog created a blanket so heavy she couldn't even see the Port

Authority, but she followed the path made by others in the snow.

Instead of huddling inside the warm terminal with the other passengers, Ana wandered out to the dock. From there, she had a vantage point of both the lighthouse and the distant shores of neighboring islands. In only a few months, she'd started to see this small patch of land as home. The lighthouse, though a depressing reminder of the crimes committed there, had become a project dear to her. The people of Summer Island accepted her. And she had finally given her heart away.

She'd leave her heart behind along with everything else.

As Ana diverted her gaze back toward the Atlantic, she drew in one last, salty breath. She held it in, and closed her eyes, convincing herself there was no other choice.

With a startling note of finality, she understood she'd also left the last of her hope with Finn. This trip home wasn't a reprieve, but the beginning of the end.

A small whistle sounded, and passengers filed out of the building, hurrying through the cold.

"Courage," Ana whispered, as she stepped carefully toward the ship, and the encroaching darkness.

Ana is headed home to New Orleans. Although she doesn't yet know it, Finn isn't far behind. But what happens when she shows up on the doorstep of the man who never wanted to speak to her again? What will she do when she realizes this "trouble" he's gotten himself into is so much more?

Don't miss a minute. Download *The Illusions of Eventide.* today.

Can't wait? Read further for an excerpt.

# THE ILLUSIONS OF EVENTIDE EXCERPT

Living no longer held much interest for Nicolas Deschanel.

This realization came amidst a rare instance of clarity for him. He couldn't pinpoint the exact moment when it initially crossed his mind, or when it moved from a whim to a done deal. Like most things in his life, it didn't occur to him slowly. The idea didn't evolve so much as appear, although looking back, every moment leading him here essentially shouted the same forgone conclusion.

He was only numbly aware of his plan as he gassed up the Porsche, packing a small leather bag, carefully nesting inside the box housing his father's handgun. Even the drive to Deschanel Island on New Year's Day was free of interesting revelations. If he were the insightful type, Nicolas might have started putting the puzzle pieces together sooner. He'd have seen the sojourn to his family's small Gulf island wasn't just another spur-of-the-moment getaway. He'd have understood this was more than Deschanel spontaneity.

There were plenty of assholes who expected something like this from him years ago, after the accident that killed off most of his family.

He grew up with four half-sisters, each products of his father's inability to stop rutting with his son's French nanny. Sisters his father loved far more than he ever loved his only son. This didn't bother Nicolas the way it should have. He grew up doing whatever he pleased, whenever he pleased, however he pleased, and there was no one who cared enough to stop him. Even his own mother, who he'd loved despite her faults, was too self-absorbed in misery of her own creation to tend to his emotional needs.

What should have been an exclamation point in his life was, in reality, more of a footnote. His entire family—except his youngest sister, Adrienne—died in a car accident deep in bayou country. At the ever-so-tender age of twenty-one, Nicolas had faced unfathomable tragedy. Most of the family biddies were on edge, waiting for him to do something characteristically selfish like drink himself into oblivion and walk down the Mississippi River levee naked.

He was too stubborn to give the Deschanel Sewing Circle the satisfaction of being right. Besides, he'd already done his share of drinking naked on the levee.

He could think of far more creative ways to go off the deep end.

It was easier to let them believe he didn't care. He'd loved his father, even if he'd been an insufferable prick. He'd loved his conniving mother, even if it was her fault Charles excluded Nicolas. And he'd loved his half-sisters too, though he suspected they never knew it.

His illusion was very convincing. He should've been on suicide watch then, the subject of everyone's thoughts and prayers. The kitchen at *Ophélie* should've been swimming with shitty casseroles. No one ever saw Nicolas mourn. They mistook his lack of tears for apathy. The ones who did come by, like Aunt Colleen, Uncle Augustus, even Aunt Elizabeth, he drove away with convincing claims of apathy.

But Nicolas did grieve. He grieved for what he *could* have had, but never did. And now, never would.

But this wasn't why he went to Deschanel Island to die. It had nothing to do with some repressed grief or inexorable loneliness stemming from a crappy upbringing or his family's accident. That was almost a decade ago. He'd experienced very little heartache in his life since, and despite his often dysfunctional rearing, he'd never been lonely. Until about a month ago, he was happy.

Nicolas knew what people thought of him. That his partying, womanizing, and travels, passing from one experience to another, were just replacements for the lack of sincere affection in his life. He let people believe that because it sounded a lot less fucked up than just admitting he preferred his lifestyle to normalcy. He loved excess. He loved money. He loved women.

Of course, it was *love*, and his screwed up definition of it, which inevitably brought him to where he was now.

His family had owned the small island off the Gulf Coast of Louisiana for many years. Since before he was born, but how long exactly he really didn't know, or care. What he did know was that it was small, private, and he'd taken steps to ensure he'd be the only living soul there.

There were five houses altogether on Deschanel Island, all owned by the Deschanel estate. Rentals, mainly, although there'd be no tenants at all now, as Nicolas had been very clear with his agent he wanted the island to himself until the end of January. He didn't know how long it would take him to sort his shit out, but he definitely didn't want company.

Of course, he didn't consciously acknowledge his intentions when he made these plans.

Neither Oz nor Ana had been surprised at his decision to go away for a while. Guilt, most likely.

"You do realize there'll be no women, and no booze, correct?" Oz had said. Nicolas resented him for thinking they'd come to the point where jokes were okay again. *Newsflash, asshole: I still hate you.*

Ana had been less flippant about it, instead sending

him a brief email with the line: *Oz told me what's going on. This isn't like you.* No, she hadn't earned the right to have an opinion about his life again, either. That email, like all the others she'd written to Nicolas since he'd left her to her new life in Maine, went unanswered and promptly deleted.

Why he continued to humor Oz, but not Ana, was somewhat of a mystery, even to him. He only knew he felt the need to punish her more, because her actions broke his heart the most.

But they could *both* go straight to hell, as far as Nicolas was concerned. If it weren't for them, he wouldn't be sitting in his parents' beach house with his father's .357 on his lap.

The only two people Nicolas had ever cared about—the only two people in the world who he knew cared about him in return—were now the only two people in the world he wanted nothing to do with. But, like a chump, he continued letting things go on in their vaguely passive manner. Continued his surface-level discussions with Oz, and resisted the urge to reply to Ana's tentative emails with an award-winning rant. Continued pretending, superficially, he was over what they'd done.

Storm clouds formed over the crystal blue water. It was too late in the season for hurricanes, but a winter storm in the Gulf could be nasty, too. He supposed he could wait until tomorrow to do the deed. It wasn't like he was on a damn schedule.

Nicolas ran his fingers over the cold steel of his father's gun. He actually had to look online to figure out how to shoot the cursed thing. Oz knew about guns. Hell, he'd handled one like a pro not so long ago, back when everyone's world started to fall apart.

Why did Oz have to unburden his conscience on him? If ignorance was bliss, Nicolas had lived an entire life of utopia. He was perfectly happy not knowing a goddamn bit about anything. He liked that his only concern in the world was whether to spend Christmas in Switzerland, or France. He didn't care what his apathy said about him, because he usually didn't give a damn what others did with their lives, either.

Knowing about Oz and Ana changed everything. Now that he knew, the rug had been pulled out from underneath his hazy, fantastical world, and he was left standing on a foundation of crumbling sand.

He sent a text message to Oz the first night. He knew he shouldn't, but it was an old habit, and old habits had always been hard for him to break. *You said to tell you when I made it to the island. Here you go, asshole.*

Oz responded almost immediately. *Thanks for your endearing note. Enjoy your self-induced solitude, Thoreau.*

Nicolas grinned, then kicked himself for it. This is how they'd talked to each other for years, for as long as they'd been friends. Hell, all their lives. Nicolas had loved Oz like his own brother. They *were* brothers, if you considered he'd married Nicolas' half-sister Adrienne.

Oz had been martyring himself on Adrienne's behalf for years, and they were finally together, and happy. At least, Nicolas thought he was happy. All happiness came at a price, and Oz had paid for his, the way everyone does to have the things they want most in life. Adrienne had paid, too.

Nicolas knew Oz didn't deserve a text, didn't deserve the peace of mind. He didn't even get credit anymore for his care of Adrienne, after what he'd done to her. If Nicolas hadn't loved his sister, he might've told her all about what her husband had been up to with her cousin. But he did love her, so he didn't.

Nicolas didn't know how to see Oz through this new, darker lens. What he'd done was fucking terrible. Nicolas' heart, that cold, dark organ renting space in his chest, had been torn asunder by it. But somewhere deep down, he also knew Oz was the best man he'd ever known. Those perspectives were warring in his head, constantly. Reasoning shit out was not something he enjoyed under any conditions.

A conversation he had, years ago with Ana, suddenly popped into his head. About a year after his family's accident, she'd claimed he could control his reaction to any situation, with practice.

*That's some bullshit*, he'd said.

*Is it?*

*If it were true, you wouldn't be such a raving basket-case*, he'd countered.

*If it* weren't *true, you'd have never survived the demise of your family*, she said, bluntly, right to the point as always.

*Explain.*

*You don't actually believe it didn't bother you?*

*No, Ana, I really didn't give a fuck*, he'd said, though they both knew that was patently untrue.

*No. You quite clearly decided not to give a fuck, and therefore, a fuck was not given.*

Of course, Nicolas resented her insinuation he was being stingy with his fucks, and he told her so. They'd debated it for another hour or so, before she'd conceded —knowing she was right— and he'd won—knowing this particular victory was hollow.

But sitting there, watching the Gulf tides, feeling the brisk, cool air tug at his jacket, Nicolas knew she'd been wrong all along. If he could control how he felt about this situation, he'd have forgiven her and Oz both, and all would be well. He'd be off to Greece for the winter, beautiful but unmemorable women on each arm, not a care in the world.

Blissfully ignorant.

Don't miss a minute. Download *The Illusions of Eventide* today.

# ALSO BY SARAH M. CRADIT

## KINGDOM OF THE WHITE SEA

### Kingdom of the White Sea Trilogy

The Kingless Crown

The Broken Realm

The Hidden Kingdom

### The Book of All Things

The Raven and the Rush

The Sylvan and the Sand

The Altruist and the Assassin

The Melody and the Master

The Claw and the Crowned

## THE SAGA OF CRIMSON & CLOVER

### The House of Crimson and Clover Series

The Storm and the Darkness

Shattered

The Illusions of Eventide

Bound

Midnight Dynasty

Asunder

Empire of Shadows

Myths of Midwinter

The Hinterland Veil

The Secrets Amongst the Cypress

Within the Garden of Twilight

House of Dusk, House of Dawn

Midnight Dynasty Series

A Tempest of Discovery

A Storm of Revelations

A Torrent of Deceit

**The Seven Series**

1970

1972

1973

1974

1975

1976

1980

**Vampires of the Merovingi Series**

The Island

and more

**The Dusk Trilogy**

St. Charles at Dusk: The Story of Oz and Adrienne

Flourish: The Story of Anne Fontaine

Banshee: The Story of Giselle Deschanel

**Crimson & Clover Stories**

Surrender: The Story of Oz and Ana

Shame: The Story of Jonathan St. Andrews

Fire & Ice: The Story of Remy & Fleur

Dark Blessing: The Landry Triplets

Pandora's Box: The Story of Jasper & Pandora

The Menagerie: Oriana's Den of Iniquities

A Band of Heather: The Story of Colleen and Noah

The Ephemeral: The Story of Autumn & Gabriel

Bayou's Edge: The Landry Triplets

**For more information, and exciting bonus material, visit www.sarahmcradit.com**

# ABOUT THE AUTHOR

Sarah is the USA Today and International Bestselling Author of over forty contemporary and epic fantasy stories, and the creator of the Kingdom of the White Sea and Saga of Crimson & Clover universes.

Born a geek, Sarah spends her time crafting rich and multilayered worlds, obsessing over history, playing her retribution paladin (and sometimes destruction warlock), and settling provocative Tolkien debates, such as why the Great Eagles are not Gandalf's personal taxi service. Passionate about travel, she's been to over twenty countries collecting sparks of inspiration, and is always planning her next adventure.

Sarah and her husband live in a beautiful corner of SE Pennsylvania with their three tiny benevolent pug dictators.

www.sarahmcradit.com

www.ingramcontent.com/pod-product-compliance
Lightning Source LLC
Chambersburg PA
CBHW020332310726
48979CB00015B/2342/J

* 9 7 8 1 9 5 8 7 4 4 0 1 7 *